GIRLFRIEND

I FORGIVE YOU

GIRLFRIEND I FORGIVE YOU

A Chronicle of a Young Woman's Journey to Wholeness

Bessie Stewart-Banks

Conscious of the Heart Publishing

Atlanta

GIRLFRIEND I FORGIVE by Bessie Stewart-Banks

Published by: Conscious of the Heart Publishing, LLC
P.O. Box 1452
Redan, Georgia 30074

Editor: Danielle Rome-Briggs
Cover design: sheergenius
Author's photo: Andrea Shedrick Photography
andreashedrick@att.net

ISBN-13: 978-0-578-46237-0 (Paperback)

Library of Congress Card Number: 2019902030

Printed in the United States of America

I dedicate this book to every young woman who has ever felt worthless and believed that she did not deserve to have good things happen to her in life and, as a result, she settled for less than God's best. I say to you, arise and shine beautiful butterfly, you are wonderful and worthy to receive all the goodness that our Heavenly Father has to offer you in life.

Love and Peace,

Bessie

Acknowledgments

Special thanks to Danielle Rome-Briggs for collaborating with Conscious of the Heart Publishing to provide your editing expertise to ensure that this book would be the best work it could be. Thank you to my son, Eric- for being my third eye and double checking my work.

Introduction

As a young girl transitions into womanhood, she will be confronted with a series of decisions that she will be forced to make. Some of her decisions will strongly impact her physical, emotional, mental and spiritual development and may inadvertently alter the course of her life.

The choices a young woman will make over a lifetime will be viewed by her parents as unfavorable and unbeneficial. More than likely, her parents will be hesitant to accept her decision, because they feel her choice will take her down a road to self-destruction. Such sentiment occurred to a young woman named Jasmine Sawman.

Jasmine is the youngest of three children and has always lived a protected and sheltered life. Jasmine has two older sisters, Ashley and Allison, and there is a five-year age gap between them. Jasmine's parents, Carl and Peggy Sawman, are a well-known and respected church-going couple from Swainsboro, Georgia.

Mr. and Mrs. Sawman are both educators and have strong ties to their small and close-knit community. The Sawmans have always taught their daughters the importance of developing a personal relationship with Jesus Christ and before making any major decision in their life to seek God's counsel. Although the Sawmans are devout Christians they give their daughters the freedom, with some restraints, to live as normal teenagers.

The Sawman girls are not allowed to date until they turn eighteen and when they reach that age and begin dating, they are expected to bring the young man home to meet their parents. The Sawman daughters are also not allowed to wear make-up, revealing clothing or get any type of tattoo.

Additionally, Jasmine and her sisters are expected to maintain good grades while in school, so they will have a better chance of getting scholarships to pay for college. Peggy and Carl Sawman imposed these rules on their daughters because they did not want them to make the wrong choices that would destroy their lives.

For years the expectations that Peggy and Carl set for their daughters seemed to be reasonable and attainable because their older daughters, Ashley and Allison, successfully graduated from both high school and college at the top of their classes and were able to land jobs with two of the most well-known Fortune 500 companies in the technology industry.

However, the rules that the Sawmans have expected their daughters to abide by will soon be challenged when Jasmine begins her freshman year at Mountain View High School. All the principles that Peggy and Carl have cherished, lived and instilled in their daughters will soon come under fire and push them to their limit. The sudden shift in their youngest daughter's behavior will cause the Sawmans to second guess their parenting style.

The path that Jasmine chooses to travel in her life will not only challenge and test her parents faith in God but will leave her unrecognizable to her loved ones, especially her parents. The various experiences and lessons that await Jasmine, based on her choices, will not only revolutionize her outlook on life, but it will force her to return to her first love.

Everything that her parents taught her and her sisters since they were small children will be tested, especially building a personal relationship with God and keeping that relationship with him first place in her life.

METAMORPHOSES OF A YOUNG GIRL

Transformation Derives from
The Choices We Make in Life

CHAPTER 1

It's the beginning of the school year and Jasmine has matriculated smoothly into her new role as a high school student at Mountain View High School. She has successfully maintained an "A" average in all her classes and has gained some new friends. It is unusual for Jasmine to befriend others because most of the time she keeps to herself. But now that she is in high school things have changed.

One of the people that Jasmine has met is Dontrelle Martin, they met in science class. Dontrelle is not the typical person that Jasmine is accustomed to hanging around. Dontrelle is somewhat of a class clown and has been classified by many of his teachers and peers as a trouble maker. Dontrelle always seems to cause disturbances in the classroom while his teachers are trying to teach. On several occasions he has pulled practical jokes on his classmates and teachers.

Even though many of the students and staff members at Mountain View tend to avoid interaction with Dontrelle, Jasmine, on the other hand, is always eager to see him every chance she gets. Jasmine is captivated by his good looks and bad boy demeanor. It is understandable that Jasmine would have such an infatuation with Dontrelle since she is not allowed to date until she turns eighteen years old. Ironically, Jasmine is only fifteen years old and too young to date according to her parent's rules.

What is more important than Jasmine being too young to date, she is naïve. Jasmine does not realize that the bad boy demeanor that Dontrelle portrays while at school and around his classmates is only a mask to the truth. The rough and ruthless behavior that Dontrelle wants everyone to believe is not who he really is; it's a cover up to hide the truth that he is a wounded young man who had to grow up fast to survive his home environment.

No one at school, not even Jasmine, knows that he has been held back in the 10th grade twice, reads at a third-grade level, and sells drugs to help his grandmother support his younger siblings since his father went to prison for the murder of his mother.

He also has a baby on the way with a girl who attends a private school for girls. With all the dysfunction that Dontrelle has going on in his life he has no choice but to portray a persona that is tough and hard, otherwise he won't last in his neighborhood or in the drug trade.

Nonetheless, as the school year progresses, and without her parent's knowledge, Jasmine begins to spend more and more time with Dontrelle during and after school. Jasmine and Dontrelle spend so much time together that everyone at school believes that they are a couple not realizing that they are just friends. It would seem as though everywhere Dontrelle went Jasmine was tagging along behind him like a lovesick puppy.

Eventually after spending so much time with one another, Jasmine and Dontrelle's friendship transposes into that of a girlfriend and boyfriend relationship. Although, Jasmine understands that the relationship she and Dontrelle have formed goes against all the rules and standards her parents have established for their daughters to follow, she ignores them because she really likes Dontrelle and wants to be with him.

As well as meeting Dontrelle, Jasmine meets Sheila Richardson in math class. Shelia is another person that Jasmine is not accustomed to hanging around. Sheila is loud, opinionated and viewed by everyone at school as a bully. Like Dontrelle, no one knows that Sheila comes from a dysfunctional home environment, one that includes an alcoholic mother and a father who is a drug addict.

Because of the way that Jasmine has been raised by her parents, to treat others with kindness and respect, her friendship with Sheila blossoms and they soon become best friends. Jasmine and Sheila's friendship is so close most of the people at school think they are sisters.

One day while hanging out at the mall with Sheila, Jasmine notices Dontrelle and decides to go over to him to say hello and give him a hug. When Jasmine returned to where Sheila was standing, Sheila said to her, "Girl what are you doing? Why did you just give the biggest loser and trouble maker at school a hug?"

Jasmine quickly responded to Sheila with a sly comment," it's none of your business, why I spoke to Dontrelle or gave him a hug. Why do you wanna know anyway?", Jasmine replied.

"Well, I thought I would ask because he does live in my neighborhood and he's no good, especially for someone like you," Sheila responses to Jasmine.

"Sheila what do you mean someone like me?", Jasmine asked.

"Jasmine I don't mean anything, I'm just looking out for you. You know we like sisters and I don't want nothing bad to happen to you," Sheila answered.

"There you go Sheila, sounding just like my parents."

"At least you got parents who care about you and what you do. Some people like me, don't have that. You should be thankful that anyone cares about your little dumb butt," Sheila replied.

"Sheila since that's the way you feel about me and my decision to like and date Dontrelle, we don't have to be friends anymore. I don't want to waste your time with hanging out with a dumb butt like me."

"Jasmine, girl you know that's not what I mean! But what I do mean and believe is that Dontrelle is not the boy for you. Jasmine you don't know him like I do. You don't even see how dating him is starting to change you and our friendship."

"Dating Dontrelle is not changing our friendship. Our friendship is changing because you are too nosey. I believe you are jealous of my relationship with him."

After hearing that statement Sheila turned and walked away from Jasmine and yelled out loud, "do what you want but when he does something stupid, like cheat on you, don't come crying to me. And by the way for your information, I don't like or date losers who sell drugs!"

Stunned by Sheila's response, Jasmine turned and walked away in the opposite direction wondering why Sheila reacted the way she did to her.

CHAPTER 2

Several months had lapsed since the heated argument between Jasmine and Sheila at the mall. During this time span they haven't spoken to one another. However, this soon changes when one day Jasmine decides she wants to attend a house party with Dontrelle at his friend Marcus' house. Jasmine had a problem, it was a school night and she knew that her parents would not allow her to be out passed her curfew unless it was school related.

Jasmine also knew she would need an alibi to cover up the fact that she was not going to be doing anything pertaining to school because she was really planning on attending the party with Dontrelle. So, Jasmine decided to give Sheila a call despite the fact they hadn't spoken to one another in months.

As Jasmine dialed Sheila's number she thought to herself, *"I hope Shelia forgives me and will help me by being my alibi."* Hello, Sheila, I hope I'm not bothering you."

"Hi Jasmine and what do you want?" "Why do you sound like you are angry or something?"

"Well, maybe because it has been over three months since I've heard from you. I know you haven't been that busy where you couldn't call me. You don't even bother to speak to me at school. What, your little boyfriend dumped you?"

"No, that's not it, Sheila. I just wanted to call you to see what's up with you and if we are okay since the argument we had at the mall."

There was a long pause. Finally, Jasmine said something to keep the conversation going and to convince Sheila to be her alibi if her parents should call her while she was out with Dontrelle. "Hey, Sheila are you there?"

"Yeah, I'm here and I am curious as to why you're calling me now out of the blue."

"Well, I called you to see how you were doing but I also wanted to know if you would do me a favor?"

Sheila angrily replies, "A favor for you, are you kidding me? After all this time you call only to ask me to do something for you?"

"I know you're mad at me and I don't blame you. I'm sorry for everything I said to you that day at the mall and getting upset with you for being concerned about me."

"What about not calling me for the last three months?", Sheila asked.

"I'm sorry about that too, I hope you can forgive me and do this one favor for me. Pleassee!"

Sheila hesitantly responds, "You know I can't stand you right now but okay, what is it you need me to do?"

"Dontrelle and I are going to his friend Marcus' house for a party tomorrow night and I'm going to tell my parents that I will be at your house, helping you study for a math exam that's coming up on Friday. All I need you to do is to be my alibi if my parents should call to verify that I am helping you study," Jasmine explained.

The conversation between Jasmine and Sheila lasted for another five minutes before Sheila agreed to be an alibi for Jasmine. "What's up with you and this boy Dontrelle? Why are you suddenly lying to your parents about where you are and what you are doing? I don't like him," Sheila exclaimed.

"Sheila how can you say you don't like Dontrelle, when you don't even know him?", Jasmine asked.

"I don't know him personally, but I do know what he does in my neighborhood. That makes me not like him. On top of what he does, look how you're changing since you started hanging around him." "I haven't changed that much," Jasmine responded.

"Really Jasmine? You haven't changed? Why do you want me to lie to your parents about you helping me to prepare for a math test to cover up the fact that you will be at a party with Dontrelle? Tell me that?" Sheila presses her point with, "Well, what do you have to say Jasmine, have you changed or not?"

There was a long pause before Jasmine responded to Sheila. After about three minutes of silence Jasmine finally responded to Sheila's question. "To answer your question Sheila, I don't think I've changed at all."

"You know what, there is no need for me to continue this conversation with you about your relationship with Dontrelle because it is going nowhere. If you want to mess up your life dating him, then that's your problem. And if you want to lie to your parents, then that's fine too. But I won't lie for you," Sheila replied.

"Okay, Sheila. I'm sorry you feel the way you do. I hope we can remain friends even though you don't like my relationship with Dontrelle." "Hmm, I guess," Sheila answered disgustedly. "Alrighty, Sheila I'll talk to you later. Love you girl."

Jasmine was seemingly not affected by how the conversation between herself and Sheila panned out, not even with the fact that she could not gain her as an alibi. So, she had to find another way to go with Dontrelle to Marcus' party without her parents discovering what she was really doing on a school night, there had to be another plan.

Jasmine had to devise one quick because it was Tuesday and the party was in two days, on Thursday night. Surprisingly, Jasmine was able to formulate a plan that would yield no suspicion from her parents as to what she would be doing on a school night passed her curfew.

Jasmine's backup plan involved telling her parents that the Caldwell's neighbors, who lived down the street from their house, needed her to babysit for them while they went on a dinner date to celebrate their anniversary.

Jasmine thought to herself, *"This plan has to work, if not I won't be able to meet up with Dontrelle at Marcus' party."*

Nonetheless, the day had arrived, and it was time for Jasmine to put her plan into action. As soon as she got home from school and just before her parents arrived home from work, Jasmine packed the clothes that she was going to change into when she reached Marcus' house.

Shortly thereafter, Mr. & Mrs. Sawman arrived home and asked Jasmine what time she had to be at the Caldwell's house. Jasmine informed her parents that she had to be at the Caldwells around six o'clock. At the time of the Sawman's inquiry it was about 4:30 p.m.

As time passed Jasmine became antsy and as not to spark her parent's suspicion, she decided to leave the house earlier than expected by telling them that she was going to stop by the corner store to pick up some snacks before she went to the Caldwells. Jasmine gathered her things and told her parents that she was headed out and would call them once she made it to the Caldwells.

As she was leaving the house her cell phone rang. It was Dontrelle on the phone. "Hey Jazz, you on your way?", Dontrelle inquired.

"Yes, I just left the house and I should be at Marcus's house in about twenty-five minutes," Jasmine replied. "Why so long?", Dontrelle commented. "Well, I am walking you know." "Okay, call me when you are getting closer."

Ten minutes had elapsed since Jasmine left her house. She received another phone call. "Jazzy," the voice on the other end of the phone responded. The voice was that of Peggy Sawman. "Yes, mom," Jasmine replied.

"Where are you?" asked her mother. "Did you forget I told you that I was going to stop by the corner and pick up some snacks before I went over to the Caldwell's house to babysit? Why are you always checking up on me?", Jasmine exclaimed.

"Honey, I'm sorry that you feel we are overprotective of you but so much is happening in the world and your father and I just want to make sure you are safe. So, what time do you think you will be heading home from the Caldwells," she inquired.

"Mr. and Mrs. Caldwell said they should return from their dinner date no later than 11:00 p.m." Jasmine informed her mother.

"Okay, but you know that's pass your curfew," she explained to Jasmine. There was a long sigh before Jasmine responded, "I know mom."

"Well, I guess that will be alright since you are just down the street. I don't want to take up anymore of your time, be careful coming home and if you need me or your father to pick you up make sure to call one of us. Love you and see you when you get home tonight."

As soon as Jasmine told her mother good-bye and hung up the phone she arrived at Marcus' house. Jasmine and Dontrelle, embracing one another, begin to laugh and say, *"It worked, the plan worked!"*

Meanwhile, Peggy had no idea that Jasmine did not go to the corner store to get snacks nor did she go to the Caldwell's house to babysit their twin boys, but she was with Dontrelle partying at Marcus' house. It was apparent that Jasmine's plan worked because she was able spend the entire evening with Dontrelle at Marcus' house party without her parents ever finding out that she was never at the Caldwells babysitting.

Nevertheless, the peaceful household and the picturesque family of the Sawmans, that many people in the community had admired for years, was about to come to a screeching halt. Jasmine's secret relationship continued with Dontrelle and her behavior diminished to a level of rudeness, disrespect, and promiscuity. Jasmine's behavior led her into a place in life where she was unrecognizable by her parents, close friends or even herself.

THE CHANGE

Not All Change Is Good Change

CHAPTER 3

Jasmine started spending her time with Dontrelle and due to her association with him, her parents had noticed a change in her demeanor. Jasmine's behavior had changed so drastically at home and school that she was no longer the studious and well-mannered young lady that everyone had been accustomed to seeing.

Jasmine's behavior changed to the point that she was now lying more and more to her parents, skipping school, being rude and disrespectful to every adult she met and dressing provocatively.

Based on the change in their daughter's behavior, Peggy and Carl had begun to question why Jasmine had become someone that they barely recognized. The Sawmans had no clue that Jasmine's alternated behavior stemmed from her affiliation with Dontrelle, the person she was secretly dating behind their back.

Jasmine's relationship with Dontrelle went against all the rules that her parents had established for their children to follow and uphold. Because of their concern over Jasmine's recent change in behavior, they decided to call a family meeting to find out exactly what had been going on in her life.

"Jasmine, can you please come downstairs your father and I would like to speak with you," Peggy exclaimed.

In response to her mother Jasmine yelled back, "Not right now mom, I'm busy doing something."

After hearing how Jasmine responded to his wife, Carl intervened and sternly informs Jasmine in a stern voice, "young lady you heard your mother, get down here. Whatever you are doing up there can wait. Get downstairs right now and I mean right now!"

In midst of yelling back and forth with their daughter, Peggy and Carl have no idea that Jasmine is not busy doing anything but is on the telephone with Dontrelle making plans to sneak out of the house and meet up with him later that night. "Jasmine, did you hear me? We are still waiting, get down here now," her asserted. Jasmine replies, "Dang, I heard you the first time."

After hearing the seriousness in her father's voice, Jasmine told Dontrelle that she would have to call him back once she found out what her parents wanted with her. Jasmine hangs up the telephone and preceded downstairs to her parents. "Yes, what ya'll want with me?"

Stunned, her mom replies, "Don't you take that tone of voice with us. Who do you think you are talking to that way? Jasmine what has gotten into you lately? You have been so disrespectful to your father and me. Your grades have gone down. You're rude to your teachers. And where did you get those clothes in your room? We certainly didn't buy them for you."

"Ugh, that's why you called me downstairs, to get into my business?"

"I don't know what has gotten into you lately but whatever it is, it better stop, today! Because if you get sassy with me or mother again, some changes are going to take place around here and trust me, you are not going to like them," her dad stated.

In a muttered voice Jasmine responded, "ya'll get on my nerves, I can't never do anything around here." "What did you say?", her mother asked. "Nothing," Jasmine answered. "I thought so."

Her dad interjected into the conversation by saying, "Jasmine we didn't call you down here to argue with you, we are just concerned about the recent change in your behavior. Are you being bullied or anything?"

"No, I'm not being bullied. I just want some more freedom. You two are so over protective and you are smothering me. I feel like I don't have a real life as a teenager like everyone else at my school. Your rules are too strict. I am not allowed to have a boyfriend until I turn eighteen and even then, the boy I choose to date must meet with your approval. I'm tired of all of your rules."

Jasmine answered, "Well, that doesn't explain why you have become so disrespectful to me, your father and teachers at school, or why your grades have gone down. The sudden change in the type of clothes you have been sneaking around and wearing, of which we didn't buy for you, none of this makes any sense." Said her mother, concern etched into her face.

"Your mother and I understand that you would like to have a lot more freedom but the world in which we live causes us to restrict you from doing some of the things that your friends do. That's why we set the high standards that we have for you and your sisters. We just want the very best for you girls, is that so bad Jasmine?"

Jasmine becomes distracted when she receives a text message from Dontrelle. The text message read, *"Jazz, what time are you headed my way? D"*

Needing to make a quick getaway Jasmine interjects, "Are we done here? I need to call Sheila she wants to ask me a question about tonight's homework in Algebra," Jasmine responded to her parents. Convinced that the conversation was essentially done her dad concedes.

"Go ahead and call Sheila back, but know that we are not done with this conversation young lady." "Alright, later," Jasmines responded.

Apparently, the heated discussion that ensued between Jasmine and her parents provided no explanation as of why her behavior had so drastically changed over the last few weeks. However, the Sawmans will soon find out the real reason behind their daughter's disrespectful behavior toward them.

Be that as it may, Jasmine continued corresponding with Dontrelle through text messaging telling him to give her some time to get out of the house to meet him. Jasmine texted Dontrelle, *"I'll try to meet you at Marcus' house around 6:45 p.m."*

Dontrelle responded to Jasmine's text by stating that she would need to arrive at Marcus' house no later than 6:30 p.m. for them to make the seven o'clock movie.

Jasmine replied *"okay."* After Jasmine responded to Dontrelle's text, she realized that she had less than thirty minutes to come up with a story to tell her parents to get out of the house and meet him at Marcus' house.

Several minutes had passed before Jasmine could devise a plan to get out of the house. Jasmine thought to herself, *"I'll tell my parents that the Sutton family who live in a neighboring community heard about how good I am with children and need me to babysit for them for a few hours while they visit with a friend in the hospital. That's it, that's what I'll tell them, and I pray to God it works."*

Jasmine proceeded to her parent's room and as she entered the room, she softly mumbled, "Mom, Dad. Can I come in and talk to you about something?" "Yes, Jasmine come in," exclaimed her father.

Concerned, her mom asked, "What is it Jasmine, you ready to tell us why your behavior has drastically changed?"

"No that's not what I want to talk to you both about, I want to ask you if I could go over to Mr. & Mrs. Sutton's house to babysit for them while they visit their friend in the hospital."

"Do you mean Jeremiah and Yvonne Sutton, who live over on Sky View Lane?", Peggy implied. "Yes, that's them," Jasmine answered.

"I thought their children were old enough to stay home by themselves," said her mom. Thinking on her feet Jasmine replied, "I guess not because they asked the Caldwells who babysat for them and they referred me to the Suttons. So, can I go?"

"Well, if it's okay with your father then it's alright with me. There's one exception, however to you going over to their house." "What's that?", Jasmine answered.

"Your father or I will have to drop you off and pick you up from the Sutton's house," said her mom. "What, you don't trust me to walk over to their house?", Jasmine responded.

"Well, a matter of fact we don't because of the way you have been behaving these few months," Carl exclaimed.

"Okay, then can we leave in a few minutes because Mr. & Mrs. Sutton want to make it to the hospital before visiting hours end," Jasmine stated. Peggy said okay and told her husband that she was taking Jasmine over to the Sutton's house and that she would return shortly.

Peggy and Jasmine left the house and in less than ten minutes they arrived at the Sutton's house. She was just about to get out of the car when Jasmine blurted out loud, "do you have to come in with me? You know I'm old enough, right?"

"Well, I guess not. Tell the Suttons your father and I said hello," she replied. As Jasmine proceeded to get out of the car, her mother reminded her, "don't forget to call your father or me when you are ready to be picked up." "Okay, bye," Jasmine responded.

As she drove away, Jasmine stood on the curb in front of the Sutton's house waving bye to her mother hoping that she would soon leave the area so that she could run to Marcus' house to meet Dontrelle and they make it to the movies on time. Within minutes of her mother leaving the Sutton's neighborhood, Jasmine ran five blocks to Marcus' house.

When Jasmine arrived at Marcus' house she was greeted by Dontrelle with a hug and a kiss. As soon as they embraced one another Jasmine blurted out loud, "I thought my mother would never leave the Sutton's neighborhood."

"Well, I'm glad that you finally made it. Let's go so we won't be late to the movies," Dontrelle replied.

Jasmine and Dontrelle arrived at the movies just as the movie trailers began playing. Although, the movie theater was nearly full, they managed to find seats in the top section of the theater somewhat away from everyone else.

Throughout the entire movie Jasmine had no clue that Dontrelle was making sexual advances toward her because her thoughts were on how she was going to make it back to the Sutton's neighborhood before her parents discovered that she didn't have a babysitting job.

Regardless, she was out on a date with Dontrelle. When the movie ended Jasmine proceeded to rush out of the theater but before she could get far Dontrelle grabbed her by the arm and asked her," Hey, Jazz what's the rush, I thought we were goin' to hang out at Marcus' house a bit before you headed back to the Sutton's neighborhood to meet your parents?"

"Dontrelle, you know why I'm rushing. I'm trying to get back to the Sutton's neighborhood before my parents realize that I lied to them and that I didn't have a babysitting job."

"Didn't you tell me that you were tired of your parents smothering you with their rules and the way they treat you like a baby?", Dontrelle asked.

Jasmine thought about what Dontrelle said to her and responded hesitantly with a yes." "Well let's go," he said, leading her away reassuringly.

As Jasmine walked with Dontrelle back to Marcus's house, she had no idea that her Aunt Pearl saw her walking with him. When Dontrelle and Jasmine arrived at Marcus' house, they walked into the house and Jasmine noticed that Marcus was not at home.

Dontrelle, I thought we were going to hang out with Marcus?", Jasmine stated.

"I didn't tell you that Marcus was going to be home. I told you that I wanted to hang out with you at his house. What, you scared to be alone with me?", Dontrelle asked slyly.

"No, that's not it. I mean, I just thought we were going to hang out with Marcus, that's all," Jasmine replied.

"Jasmine, we are wasting too much time talking about if Marcus is at home or not. Don't you want to spend time with me?", Dontrelle exerted.

"Yes, Dontrelle. You right. We have spent too much time talking about Marcus," Jasmine exclaimed.

As Dontrelle proceeded to the living room to sit down on the sofa, he motioned for Jasmine to sit next to him. When Jasmine joined Dontrelle on the sofa, he began kissing and feeling all over her body. Since Jasmine did not feel like she was pretty enough to attract any other boy and the fact she was infatuated with Dontrelle, she didn't stop him. Before she knew it, Jasmine ended up having sex with Dontrelle forgetting all about the principles her parents taught her and even meeting them at the Sutton's house.

Meanwhile, Aunt Pearl telephoned her sister Peggy to find out when she and her husband began allowing Jasmine to date boys? "Hey sis, this Pearl. Girl, I know this you, what's up?", Peggy replied.

"I was calling to find out when did you and Carl start allowing Jasmine to date boys?", Pearl inquired.

"What do you mean, when did we start allowing Jasmine to date boys? Pearl, you know we have always told our girls that they could not date until they turned eighteen."

"Well, I thought I would call and ask because tonight I saw Jasmine walking with some strange boy over on Tinsley Street toward the movie theater."

"No, I don't think that was Jasmine because she is over at Jeremiah and Yvonne Sutton's house babysitting."

"If you say so but I could have sworn that was her walking with a boy," Pearl exclaimed.

"If it will make you feel better, I'll call the Suttons to confirm that Jasmine is at their house babysitting and call you back." Peggy exerted, fully persuaded in Jasmine's integrity.

"That's not necessary, if you say she's babysitting at the Sutton's house then we will leave it at that." Pearl replied, convinced she must have been wrong.

Although Peggy's sister Pearl insisted that it was not necessary for her to contact the Suttons to confirm that Jasmine was at their house babysitting, she started to wonder if it was Jasmine her sister had seen. Could this boy be the reason behind Jasmine's sudden behavior change. To ease her curiosity, Peggy called the Sutton's house to see if Jasmine would answer the phone but to her surprise Yvonne Sutton answered.

"Hi, Yvonne. This is Peggy. I was calling to find out if my daughter Jasmine was babysitting your kids tonight."

"Ahh no, my husband and I have been at home all night. We didn't need a babysitter for our kids."

Suddenly concerned and confused Yvonne asked, "is everything okay with Jasmine?" As to not make it apparent that she did not know where her daughter was, Peggy politely responded with a "*yes*" and thanked her for answering her call. Upon discovering that it was in fact Jasmine that Pearl saw walking with a mysterious boy, Peggy hung up the phone and immediately informed her husband of what she had just found out about their daughter.

In the meantime, Jasmine realized it was getting late and she needed to leave Marcus' house so that she could make it back to the Sutton's house to call her parents to pick her up.

As Jasmine proceeded to put her clothes on, Dontrelle rolled over off the sofa and said, "Hey girl, you leaving?"

"Yes, Dontrelle. I've already stayed longer than I was supposed to and did some other things I was not supposed to do with you. I gotta go, I'll call you tomorrow," a flustered Jasmine replied.

She rushed out of the door of Marcus' house and ran as fast as she could toward the Sutton's neighborhood. Once Jasmine got within one block of the Sutton's house, she called her parents to inform them that she was ready to be picked up. Shortly after receiving the call from Jasmine, that she was ready to be picked up, her mom arrived.

When Jasmine got in the car, she began explaining to her mother how her evening was babysitting the Sutton children, unaware that her Aunt Pearl had seen her earlier that evening, walking with Dontrelle. She had no idea that her mother had called Yvonne Sutton to confirm that she was babysitting her kids.

The entire time driving home Peggy did not say a word to Jasmine because she was angry and hurt that her daughter lied to her and husband. She did not want to say anything to Jasmine until she and her husband could confront their daughter together.

As soon as Jasmine and her mother arrived at home, her parents confronted their daughter. "Jasmine come with me into the living room. Your father and I have something to discuss with you."

"What now, I'm tired and if you forgot I do have school tomorrow," Jasmine responded.

"We don't care if you are tired, but we do care that you lied to us about having a babysitting job at the Sutton's house. And who is this mysterious boy your Aunt Pearl saw you with over on Tinsley Street?", Carl exclaimed.

Sticking to her story, Jasmine boldly exerted herself. "What are talking about, I was at the Sutton's house all night babysitting their children."

"Look Jasmine your father and I are not going to stand here and argue with you. I already spoke with Yvonne Sutton and she confirmed that you were not at her house babysitting her children. We also know you were with some boy that you know you are not allowed to date. Jasmine, since you have insisted on lying to us and being disrespectful to all adults you come in contact with, your mother and I have agreed to put you on punishment for a month. You are not to go anywhere accept to school and back home. No cellphone. No computer unless you need it to do homework," an angry and disappointed Carl replied.

"What do you mean I can't have my cellphone? That's not fair, I need my cellphone," she yelled at her parents.

"Well get used to not having it. Until your behavior improves, you won't have it. Now hand over the cellphone and go to bed," Carl replied, cutting her off.

As Jasmine walked to her room, she wondered how she was going to contact Dontrelle now that she didn't have her cellphone anymore. Then Jasmine remembered that all hope was not loss. She could still see Dontrelle at school. This is the point in Jasmine's life where her desire to be with Dontrelle and experience having a boyfriend, like all the other girls at her school, distorted her better judgement and altered the course of her life.

CHAPTER 4

It had been several weeks since Jasmine lost the privilege of having her cellphone and being able to leave the house. Yet, that had not deterred her from being disrespectful and rude toward her parents and teachers.

Jasmine not only spent more time with Dontrelle at school, but she managed to skip classes on several occasions to be with him. Jasmine's behavior continued until one day, she and Dontrelle attempted to leave school during lunch and were caught by a Campus Security Officer.

Because Jasmine was caught at school trying to leave without permission her parents were contacted. She was placed on in-school suspension. Upon being informed that their daughter attempted to skip school and was placed in-school suspension, the Sawmans both thanked school officials and told them that they would speak with her at home. When Jasmine arrived at home, she noticed that her parents were waiting for her in the living room.

"Jasmine come in the living room, your mother and I need to speak with you," her father exclaimed.

Her voice laced with annoyance, "What now?" Jasmine responded to her father.

"Jasmine, your father and I have decided that since your behavior at home and school has drastically changed and you still are hanging around some boy we don't know and didn't give you permission to date, you will no longer be attending Mountain View High. We have arranged for you to attend St. Catherine's Academy," her mother stated.

"That's an all-girls school! I don't want to go there, I'll have to make new friends all over again," Jasmine gasped angrily.

"Well, you can thank yourself for this decision. We had to do this. It was your behavior that forced us to go down this road with you," Carl said matter-of-factly.

"Can I get another chance to prove myself?", Jasmine pleaded.

"No, that's our final decision. You will have to live with it because you will start attending there next week. Now go to your room," Peggy asserted.

As Jasmine walked toward her room, she realized that it would be impossible for her to hang out with Dontrelle now that she would be attending a different high school. The next day at school Jasmine informed Dontrelle that she would no longer be attending Mountain View because her parents were making her go to St. Catherine's Academy.

Now they needed to find another way to continue to see each other. After hearing the news that Jasmine would not be going to Mountain View anymore, Dontrelle told her that it was best that they remained friends and wished her the best at her new school. Not believing what she had just heard, Jasmine began crying uncontrollably.

"What do you mean we can just be friends, I thought we were more than that?", Jasmine insisted.

"I never said you were my girlfriend. I thought you were someone cool to hang out with," Dontrelle replied.

"That's not what you told me all those times we had sex," Jasmine shouted.

Nonchalantly Dontrelle blurts back, "Jazzy you are not the first girl I told that lie to. I tell that to every girl I want to sleep with. Now if you done, I have to go."

Stunned by Dontrelle's response, Jasmine ran away distraught in the opposite direction. Overhearing what Dontrelle said to Jasmine, Sheila ran down the corridor of the freshman building after her yelling," Jasmine wait up!"

When Sheila reached where Jasmine had stopped, she said to her, "Girl stop crying. That boy is not worth shredding one tear over. Anyway, didn't I try to tell you that Dontrelle was no good and he's nothing but a dog," Sheila replied.

"Don't say that, he's just mad because after today I won't be going to school here anymore. My parents are sending me to that dumb all-girls school over on Kenbridge Boulevard," Jasmine tearfully responded. "Why are they doing that?", Sheila asked.

"They said I have to go there because my behavior at home and school has changed. Also, I got caught skipping school with Dontrelle," Jasmine answered.

"Girl, I didn't know you were doing all of that," Sheila exclaimed.

"How would you have known any of that was happening when we haven't spoken to one another in weeks," Jasmine replied. "Well, whose fault is that?", Sheila bluntly stated.

"Okay Sheila, it's my fault. Is that what you wanted me to say, it's my fault!", Jasmine yelled.

"I'm sorry, I didn't mean it was your fault. It's not your fault, it's no one's fault. You know what, let's not talk about this anymore. I know you got a lot on your mind already. Let's go to lunch before the bell rings for fifty block," Sheila answered.

As Jasmine and Sheila walked toward the cafeteria, Sheila said "You know I'm going to miss you Jasmine, you are the first real friend I've ever had."

"I'm going to miss you too Sheila. We can still be friends and hangout with each other, can't we?"

"Of course, we can. You're only going to another school. It's not like you moving away. Alright, enough with the mushy stuff. Give me a hug girl and let's get some food. With all this talking we only have ten-minutes left before the bell rings."

During lunch Jasmine and Sheila sat and reminisced about how on the first day of school they were so nervous to be in high school and did not really know anyone. They reflected on the times they hung out at the Pembroke Mall, the arguments they had and made plans to go to the movies when Jasmine was off punishment.

CHAPTER 5

Jasmine had been attending St. Catherine Academy for a month and had not made any new friends. Until one day in P.E. class she noticed a girl sitting alone on the bleacher crying. She walked over to the girl and introduced herself. "Hi, I'm Jasmine are you okay?"

Wiping tears with her hand, the girl turned toward Jasmine and said, "Yes, I'm okay my name is Angel."

"Nice to meet you Angel," Jasmine replied. The girls spent the next fifty-minutes of class talking. While talking to one another they discovered they had some things in common: they both were from Christian households, they were the youngest child in their families, and they were transferred to St. Catherine's because of their disrespectful behavior. Both girls also unknowingly have dated the same boy, Dontrelle.

Over the next several weeks Jasmine's friendship with Angel developed into a close one, so close that one day Angel confided in her. "Jasmine can I tell you something?" "Yeah, tell me what?"

"Umm, I'm pregnant and I think that if the school finds out I'll be kicked out," Angel responded. "They can't do that," Jasmine exerted.

"Yes, they can because it's written in the student code of conduct that girls who are discovered to be pregnant can no longer attend," Angel implied. "So, what are you going to do?"

"Well, first I need to tell my boyfriend and find out what he wants to do. Hey, you might know him, he goes to school over at Mountain View," Angel stated. "What's his name?", Jasmine asked. "Dontrelle Smith, most of his close friends call him *D*. Do you know him?", Angel inquired.

Shocked to hear that Angel was involved with Dontrelle and now was pregnant by him, Jasmine responded hesitantly with a *yes* as to not alarm her that she too had dated him.

"Wow, that's great you know him, so do you think he'll be happy that I'm pregnant?"

"I don't know, you'll just have to tell him and see what he says," Jasmine suggested. "What's wrong with you?"

"Nothing! Look I got to go to class I'll see you later," Jasmine responded. "Ok, talk to you later," Angel replied.

As Jasmine walked away from where Angel was standing, she wondered to herself why Sheila didn't tell her that Dontrelle had a girlfriend, since they all lived in the same neighborhood. Later that day, when Jasmine arrived home, she called Sheila to tell her what she found out about Dontrelle and to ask her why she didn't tell her that he had a girlfriend.

"Hi, Sheila this Jazz are you free to talk?" "Hey, Jasmine what's up?", Sheila exclaimed.

"I called you because I found out today that the girl I told you I met at St. Catherine's is Dontrelle's girlfriend. Why didn't you tell me about her?", Jasmine asked.

"Jasmine I tried to tell you about Dontrelle, but you didn't want to listen to me. Remember that day at the mall when we got into that big argument after I tried to tell you about the kind of person he was, and you told me that I was jealous of your relationship with him?"

"Yeah, I remember. But you still didn't tell me he had a girlfriend."

"Jasmine, I couldn't tell you Dontrelle was dating anyone because I didn't know," Sheila answered.

As their conversation continued, Sheila questioned Jasmine why she was so concerned about not knowing that Dontrelle had a girlfriend. "Jasmine, what's the big deal? Does it really matter if Dontrelle is dating that girl or not?", Shelia asked.

"Yes, it does matter because she is pregnant with his baby and I might be pregnant too."

"How is that possible when you've never had sex with Dontrelle? Wait, don't tell me you had sex with that boy!", Sheila exclaimed.

"Unfortunately, I did, several times," Jasmine responded. "When did this all happen and where was I?", Sheila asked.

"It happened during the time we were not talking to each other," Jasmine confided. "Well are you sure you pregnant or are you just saying that because you want Dontrelle to be with you and not that girl Angel?"

"No, I'm not just saying I'm pregnant. I really think that I am, I haven't had my period in two months," Jasmine responded.

"Have you taken a pregnancy test to see if you are or not?" "No, I haven't."

"Ok then, tomorrow after you get out of school meet me at the corner of Polemen and Universal and I'll go with you to the clinic to get a pregnancy test done. And Jasmine I'm sure you not pregnant, you probably just stressed out because you had to go to a new school during the middle of the semester."

"It's getting late and I still have homework to do. I'll see you tomorrow after school."

"Sheila, I hope you right that I'm just stressed out."

"Alright good night girl. Everything is going to be fine, you'll see."

The next day at school Jasmine was so preoccupied with the thought of where she was going after school that she did not pay attention in any of her classes and she completely avoided having any kind of interaction with Angel. In the haze of worry, the school day ended and as the bell rang Jasmine immediately left school to meet Sheila.

As soon as Jasmine arrived at the spot where that Sheila suggested that they met at, they walked to the free clinic. When they arrived at the clinic Jasmine checked in and was instructed by a nurse to have a seat and wait until her name was called. While they waited, Jasmine thought to herself, *"what if the test does come back that I'm pregnant, what am I going to do and how am I going to tell Dontrelle and my parents?"*

Shortly after this thought crossed her mind, a nurse called her name. As Jasmine proceeded to the walk to the back room with the nurse, she nervously looked at Sheila and whispered," Wish me luck?"

After about fifteen minutes Jasmine returned to the waiting area in tears. "What's wrong? Are you pregnant or not?", Sheila asked. Unable to speak Jasmine nodded her head to signal a yes. In response to Jasmine's nod Sheila blurted out loud, "Oh no!" and walked over to console her.

"Jasmine don't cry, everything is going to be ok. Now that you know, you need to tell Dontrelle. How pregnant are you anyway?"

Gaining her composure Jasmine informed Sheila that the nurse figured she was around eight weeks pregnant. "Do you want me to go with you over to Dontrelle's house, so you can tell him?", Sheila asked.

"No thanks, I don't feel like talking about this anymore today. I just want to go home and think about how I'm going to tell him and my parents," Jasmine responded.

"Ok, do you want me to walk with you to your house?"

"No, you don't have to I'll be fine. I just want to be alone right now. Thank you for coming with me today and being a good friend. I will call you tomorrow when I get home from school."

As Jasmine and Sheila began to walk in opposite directions, they turned and waved bye at each other. Throughout her entire walk home, Jasmine wondered to herself how Dontrelle and her parents were going to respond to the news that she was pregnant.

While walking home, Jasmine concluded that for the time being it was only necessary to tell Dontrelle that she was pregnant. Once it was decided if they would keep the baby, then her parents would be told.

When Jasmine got home, she walked passed her father without acknowledging that he was sitting at the dining room table. "Hi, Jasmine. How was your day at school?", Carl inquired. Still unaware that her father was speaking to her, Jasmine mumbled *no* and kept walking toward her room. Before Jasmine could reach her bedroom door, her father called her back to where he was sitting.

"Princess is everything alright with you?" "Yes dad, why do you ask?", Jasmine said in return.

"I asked because when you came in the house you didn't speak to me. Also, when I asked you how your day was at school you said, no. That's why I asked."

"Well, dad I had a long day at school, I'm tired and I have homework to do. Can I go now?" "Yes, you can."

As Jasmine walked back toward her bedroom, she told her father that she didn't want anything for dinner because when she was done with her homework she was going straight to bed. Her father said *"ok"* and wished her a good night. Instead of Jasmine doing her homework she got in the bed and stared at the ceiling until she fell asleep.

LOST

*Sometimes You Must Lose Your
Way to Find Your Path in Life*

CHAPTER 6

The next morning before Jasmine got up to get ready for school, she laid in her bed thinking. If she had not been so naïve and had listened to Sheila about not getting involved with Dontrelle, she wouldn't be in the predicament she was currently faced with. Jasmine then realized that it was too late to think about the should've and could've in her life. She was pregnant, and she needed to find a way to tell Dontrelle.

Not eager to face the day, Jasmine slowly got up out of her bed to start getting ready for school. While she was putting on her clothes there was a knock on her bedroom door. "Good morning Jasmine. Are you up getting ready for school?"

"Yes mom. I'm getting ready for school. I'll be downstairs in a minute." "Ok sweetie," Peggy said.

When Jasmine was done getting dress, she went downstairs. As she approached the dining room, her father instructed her to have a seat and he would bring her a plate of food. After hearing these directives from her father, Jasmine immediately responded, "I'm not that hungry this morning, I'll just grab a cup of orange juice and piece of toast."

"Jasmine is everything ok with you? You didn't eat dinner last night and now no breakfast?" As Jasmine gulped down her toast and orange juice she stated, "Yes, dad everything is ok with me. I gotta go now so I won't miss the bus."

While running out the door, Jasmine yelled back at her parents, "bye mom and dad I'll see you later!"

"What no hug or kiss?", they playfully hollered back at Jasmine.

After Jasmine had left the house, Carl questioned his wife about their daughter's recent strange behavior. "Do think Jasmine's behavior has gotten better since we sent her to St. Catherine?"

"To tell you the truth, it seems as if she has become more withdrawn. Honey that doesn't concern me as much as her not eating?", Peggy stated.

"Well I believe it's time that we get to the bottom of all these sudden behavior changes in Jasmine because none of it makes sense."

Meanwhile, as Jasmine was walking to the bus stop to catch the city bus to school, she decided to text Dontrelle, *"Hey, Dontrelle. I know we haven't talked in a while, but I need to see you. I have something very important to talk to you about. Would it be alright if I stopped by your house after school today? Please text me back if it's ok. Thanks, Jazz."*

As soon as Jasmine hit the send button her cellphone notified her that she had a message from Dontrelle, *"For what? D"*

Jasmine instantly wrote back, *"I have something to tell you and I can't do it over the phone or through text messaging. So, can I come by?"* After waiting nearly five minutes to receive a response from Dontrelle, the city bus came.

As Jasmine proceeded to get on the bus, she received a reply from Dontrelle, *"Yes you can come by, but the conversation has to be short*

because I have someone to meet at five o'clock. D"
"Ok, I'll be there and see you this afternoon."

From the moment it was confirmed that Dontrelle agreed to see her and to hear what she had to say, Jasmine could not concentrate in any of her classes until she was approached by Angel in P.E. class. "Hi Jasmine, are you ok?"

"Yeah, Angel, everything is fine. Why do you ask?"

"I ask because ever since I told you I was pregnant with my boyfriend's baby, you've have been acting weird toward me and avoiding me in P.E. class!"

"I said everything is fine with me, Angel. Look, I have a lot on mind right now, I don't have time to talk to you."

Unaware that they had been dating the same boy and now are pregnant with his baby, Angel began to tell Jasmine the reaction she received from Dontrelle, when she told him she was carrying his child.

"Well, Jasmine all I wanted to tell you is that I told my boyfriend that I was pregnant with his baby and surprisingly he was happy."

Annoyed and upset by what she had just heard, Jasmine walked away from Angel without saying a word.

As the day continued, Jasmine wondered to herself if Dontrelle would react the same way he reacted when Angel told him she was pregnant with his child. However, the moment of truth would come in less than an hour because school would be over. Jasmine spent the rest of P.E. watching the clock. After forty-five minutes had passed the school bell rang and Jasmine rushed to meet Dontrelle.

Eager to meet up with him to tell him that she was pregnant, Jasmine ran the whole way to his house. Before Jasmine knocked on Dontrelle's door, she decided to wait a few minutes to catch her breath and regain her composure. Once she felt confident enough, Jasmine proceeded to knock on the door but before she could the door opened and there stood Dontrelle.

"Hi, Dontrelle how have you been?" "Good, what is it you needed to tell me that couldn't be said over the phone or through text?" Taking a deep breath Jasmine proceeded to say, "Ok well I wanted to tell you that I'm pregnant with your baby."

When Jasmine informed Dontrelle that she was pregnant with his child he immediately denied being the father. "Jasmine, I don't know what you are talking about but that's not my baby. You need to find your baby daddy because I'm not him."

"What do you mean? This is your baby. You are the only person that I have ever had sex with. I lost my virginity to you Dontrelle! Why are you doing this to me?"

"Well, if it is mine, what do you want me to do?"

"I thought we would have it," Jasmine answered.

"No, that's not going to happen, you have to get rid of it. I already have a kid on the way with my girl," Dontrelle explained.

"Are you kidding me, you want me to have an abortion?" Jasmine questioned.

"Yes! Didn't I just tell you that I have a baby on the way with my girlfriend? And anyway, I'm only seventeen I can't be a father of two kids," Dontrelle replied.

Jasmine could not believe what she was hearing. The person she lost her virginity to and someone she defied her parent's rules to be with had now betrayed her love because of another girl she didn't know anything about until recently. Jasmine now realized that everything Sheila tried to warn her about, and her parents attempted to shelter her from was true.

The lingering question that rest on Jasmine's mind was, *"What will she do now that Dontrelle wants her to have an abortion and how will she tell her parents that she is eight weeks pregnant?"*

CHAPTER 7

It has been nearly three weeks since Jasmine told Dontrelle that she was pregnant with his baby. During this time Jasmine had not made up her mind whether she would keep her baby or not. Jasmine also had not determined if it would be necessary to tell her parents that she was pregnant.

However, if Jasmine does decide to tell her parents of her pregnancy, she will have to admit to herself that her parents were justified in their strict rules and sheltering her, and the fact that Sheila warned her about Dontrelle. No matter what choice Jasmine makes, she will need to do it soon because she is starting to show signs that she is pregnant. This is the moment that Jasmine will need to swallow her pride and get some wise counsel.

One day while talking on the phone with Sheila, Jasmine decided to tell her everything that transpired since the last time they spoke. "Hey Sheila, I'm sorry it's been awhile but can I talk to you about what's been happening with me without you being judgmental?"

"Yeah girl, you know you can tell me anything. Matter of fact, I was just thinking about you this morning and wondered what happened to you."

"Well, a lot has happened. But before I tell you what has happened in my life these last few weeks, sorry for accusing you of being jealous of my relationship with Dontrelle."

"Jasmine, you don't have to apologize to me, I know you were going through your first love phase. I told you awhile back that everything was cool between me and you."

Jasmine takes a deep breath. "Okay, don't judge me for what I'm about to tell you." Sheila's response to Jasmine was "okay, go ahead and tell me what's been going on with you."

With tears in her eyes Jasmine confessed to Sheila that she was right about Dontrelle not being good for her. "Wow, I can't believe it. You are honestly telling me that I was right about Dontrelle? That loser must have really said or done something to you that broke your heart."

"Sheila it's already hard for me to tell you that you were right about him, I don't need you to make me feel worse."

"Don't get me wrong Jasmine, I'm not trying to judge you, I'm just shocked."

"Well get ready to be shocked even more. I told Dontrelle a few weeks ago that I was pregnant with his baby and he denied being the father and told me to go and find the real baby daddy." "What? No, Dontrelle didn't!"

"Yes, he did and that's not all. He admitted to me that he had a baby on the way with his girlfriend."

"Not that girl you told me about? What's her name? Angel or something."

"Yes, Angel. But that's not all, he wants me to get an abortion. Saying that he's too young to be the father of two kids."

"He should've thought about his age when he was sleeping with the both of you without any protection. See that's why I didn't want you dating him. I knew he was no good for you!"

"Well Sheila it's too late to be mad, I need to decide if I'm going to have this baby or not. And if I do decide to keep it, I have to find a way to tell my parents that I'm pregnant with their first grandchild."

"If you want my opinion, I think you should keep it. I'll help you with providing free babysitting service. Ahh, my little niece or nephew could call me Auntie She-She," Sheila suggested.

"Ok, ok Sheila let's not go that far, I haven't decided what I'm going to do yet."

"How much time do you have to make a final decision before it's too late to have an abortion?"

"Hmm, let me count. I was eight-weeks when the lady at the free clinic told me I was pregnant and that was about three weeks ago. So that means I am around eleven weeks pregnant. I think I'm running out of time."

"Again Jasmine, I truly think you should consider having your baby. You already got one thing dangling over your head that you regret." "And what's that?", Jasmine asked.

"Uh, must I remind you, having sex with your baby's loser daddy!"

"I don't know, Sheila. I don't know if I'm ready to be a mother."

"Jasmine, I bet you didn't think like that when you were sleeping with that boy. Anyway, whatever you decide to do I will be here for you."

"Sheila, thank you so much for being a good friend, no matter how annoying your honesty is. I couldn't think of being best friends with no one else but you."

"Ah, boo! Thank you and I couldn't think of anyone I would rather be best friends with than you. We are best friends for life."

"Alright Sheila, we have been on this phone for about two-hours and I still have some homework to do. I'll call you in about two days and let you know what I've decided to do about my situation."

"Situation? Why are you suddenly referring to your pregnancy as a situation?"

"Hi dad, I'm on the phone with Sheila, I'll be off in a few minutes." Jasmine told her father.

"Oh, gotcha. Your dad must have come in your room?" "Yes, he did and I'm not quite ready to tell my parents that I'm pregnant," Jasmine stated.

"I understand. Well, I also have homework, so let me get off this phone and do it. Remember, Jasmine whatever you decide to do I'm here for you! Love you girl, bye."

Although the conversation between Jasmine and Sheila went well, Jasmine still must reveal her pregnancy to her parents. The support she receives from them will guide her decision. To get her mind off her problems, Jasmine begins to complete her social studies homework. However, before Jasmine could get into her homework, her father entered her room.

"Hello princess, I wanted to see how your day was at school."

"Hi again dad, school was okay. Why do you ask?"

"I feel as though lately you have been a bit withdrawn from your mother and me. Furthermore, your mother and I have noticed that you have put on some weight. Jasmine, we are just concerned about you."

Overwhelmed by her father's questioning and the fact that she had not told anyone except for Sheila, Jasmine suddenly blurted out loud, "I'm pregnant!"

"What did you say young lady?" "I said I'm pregnant, daddy. I've been keeping this secret from you and mommy for weeks now and I can't keep it to myself anymore." Not believing what he had just heard from his baby girl, Carl stood paralyzed in disbelief in the doorway of Jasmine's room.

"Dad, dad! Did you hear me?", Jasmine asked. "Yes Jasmine, I heard you. I can't believe what you just said. I don't know how your mother is going to react to this news."

"Do we have to tell her right now?" "Yes, we do. She has a right to know that her baby is going to have a baby."

"Well, can we please tell her tomorrow?", Jasmine asked her father.

"No, we need to tell her when she gets home from work, so we can decide how we are going to deal with this issue. Jasmine, I want you to know that no matter what choice you and the baby's father make, we love you and will support your decision."

As soon as Carl expressed this sentiment to Jasmine, the front door opened, and it was her mother. "Hello honey, I'm home!" Peggy yelled up the stairs.

"Hey sweetheart I'm upstairs in Jasmine's room. When you put your things down come to her room, we have some things to discuss with you." Carl informed his wife.

"What things?" "Ahh, I'll wait 'til you get up here to tell you."

"Is there something wrong with Ashley or Allison?", Peggy asked.

"No sweetie just come to Jasmine's room and we'll talk."

"Ok then, give me a minute to change my clothes."

While Peggy was changing her clothes, Jasmine was upstairs with her father trying to figure out the best way to tell her mother that she was pregnant. "Daddy, what do you think is the best way to tell mom I'm pregnant?" Jasmine asked.

"Jasmine, I believe you should just tell your mother that you are pregnant and not sugar coat the conversation."

"She's on her way up the stairs, so here goes nothing."

As Jasmine and her father waited patiently for Peggy to appear, they sat in silence. When Peggy did reach Jasmine's room she immediately walked over to her husband and gave him a kiss on the cheek and said, "Hey you two, what is so important you needed to talk to me as soon as I walked in the house." At this moment Jasmine stood and asked her mother to have sit next to her father.

"Ok, what's going on here? Y'all starting to worry me. Can you just tell me what it is before I have a heart attack?"

After hearing her mother's request, Jasmine began to speak but only gibberish came out of her mouth. Noticing his daughter was having trouble speaking, Carl took it upon himself to explain to his wife what the big news was. "Sweetheart, I'm about to tell you something and I want you to promise me that you will hear me out before you make any comments. Do you promise? "Yes, I promise!"

Once he was assured that his wife would cooperate, Carl began to share with her the news she had been waiting to hear. "Peggy, I found out today that we are going to be grandparents."

"How's that possible when Ashely and Allison are not married, and Jasmine is too young."

"Wait a minute, didn't you promise me that you would not interrupt while I told you the news?" "Yes, I did, I'm sorry go ahead."

"Alright, as I stated before, we are going to be grandparents and Jasmine is the one who's going to bless us with this precious gift."

Shocked by the news that her young and unwedded daughter was pregnant, Peggy spent the remainder of the evening crying, unable to speak and wondering where she and her husband went wrong as parents.

CHAPTER 8

The moon was still in the sky when a restless Peggy walked outside onto her balcony to gaze at the stars, imagining that everything that had transpired hours before was all a dream. While she stood motionless, looking at the sky, she began to ask God *"Father, where did we go wrong with raising Jasmine? Were our household rules the cause of our baby girl getting pregnant? Did we not show Jasmine enough love and attention?"*

Suddenly, Peggy's innocent questioning of God turned into anger.

"Lord, I don't understand what's going on, how could this girl end up pregnant at fifteen? How did she have time to date anyone? Uh, what was she

thinking? Did she not realize that once the administrators at St. Catherine's found out that she was pregnant they would kick her out of school? Lord, what are we going to do with this girl?"

Overhearing his wife's frustrated words from the bedroom window, Carl decided to join her out on the balcony. "Peggy who are you talking to?"

"Hi, babe I was having a conversation with God."

"Well from the bedroom it sounds like you were out here arguing with someone."

"I'm sorry, did I wake you up?" "No, I was getting up anyway to use the bathroom when I heard your voice and I decided to come and check on you. By the way, why were you speaking to God in that tone?"

"Carl, I didn't mean to sound so rash with God, but I just don't understand how Jasmine ended up pregnant after all we tried to do to prevent things like this from happening!"

"Sweetheart we can't get angry or blame God for a decision that Jasmine chose to make. Peggy, what is it that you tell your girlfriends they should do when they are confronted with a difficult issue in their family?"

"I tell them to pray and ask God for direction."

"Ok then since we are already outside standing under this beautiful sky, let's pray and seek God for his guidance on how to deal with Jasmine's pregnancy."

So, Peggy began to pray:

"Dear heavenly Father we come to you by way of your son Jesus Christ, our savior and redeemer. Father being that you are the God who sees and knows all, we humbly submit to you for your guidance on how we should deal with Jasmine's pregnancy. Father God, we realize that the act was a sin but not the precious baby that will come out of it. We pray and ask Lord, that you will grant us the wisdom on how to respond to questions when they are asked and that we remain sensitive to our daughter's feelings and supportive in whatever decision she makes. In closing but never-ending Lord Jesus let your will be done in this matter."

-Amen

As soon as Peggy finished, her husband gave her a big hug and told her what a beautiful job she had done in praying. "Now, do you feel better?"

"Yes, I do! What time is it?" "It's time for both of us to get ready for work."

"Wow, time has gone by so quick. I don't think I got any sleep at all last night." Realizing that they had less than an hour and a half before they had to be to work, Peggy and Carl began preparing themselves for the day.

Meanwhile, Jasmine was in her room waking up to a brand-new day of decisions she had to make and one of those decisions consisted of whether to have her baby or not. When Jasmine rolled over in her bed and noticed that it was almost seven o'clock, she immediately jumped up out of bed and got into the shower.

The entire time Jasmine was showering, she wondered if her parents were mad with her because of the news she shared with them the previous night. A short time later when Jasmine had completed getting dress for school, she went downstairs to eat breakfast. As Jasmine entered the kitchen, she greeted her father, "Good morning dad."

"Hi Jasmine, how are you this morning? Did you sleep well?"

"I slept okay, it was a long night though."

"Do you want some of these scrambled eggs I'm cooking for your mother?"

"No, I think I'll just have a bowl of cereal and a piece of toast. My stomach feels a bit queasy this morning."

Carl went on to ask Jasmine, "Do you think it would be wise for you to eat anything with milk? Are you sure you don't want eggs for breakfast?"

"Dad, I'm sure. I don't want to be sick at school."

"Alright have a seat and eat your cereal, I'll make you some toast."

While Jasmine sat at the kitchen table, she turned to her father and asked him, "Dad, are you and mom disappointed in me?"

"No princess, absolutely not. Why, do you ask?"

"I just feel like you both expected more out of me since Ashley and Allison managed to graduate high school and college without having kids out of wedlock."

Carl responded with his gentle wisdom, "It sounds like to me you are displeased with yourself."

As the conversation between Jasmine and Carl continued, Peggy entered the room and said," Good morning sunshine, did you sleep well?" "Yes mom, I slept well."

Turning to her husband, "Honey, what's for breakfast?"

"Have a seat. I cooked you some scrambled eggs and wheat toast." Peggy told her husband, "*thank you.*"

"Jasmine since we all are here together, I want to clear the atmosphere and say that although I feel somewhat disappointed in you, I do love you and will support whatever decision you and the baby's father decide to do." Surprised by what his wife said to their daughter, Carl shook his head in disappointment.

Meanwhile, looking down into her bowl of cereal, Jasmine took a deep sigh and began to cry uncontrollably.

"Oh baby, I didn't say that to upset you. I just wanted to address the awkwardness that was in the air."

Realizing that she hurt Jasmine's feelings, Peggy offered an apology for the harsh words she used with speaking to her, "please forgive me if I hurt your feelings." After Peggy apologized, she leaned over toward Jasmine and gave her a hug.

"Now, now you two stop it with all that hugging, we all have only five minutes to leave the house, so I suggest you both eat up."

Peggy quickly ate her food and as she prepared to leave for work, she asked Jasmine if she wanted her to drop her off at school. To eliminate the possibility of going to school upset, Jasmine opted for her father to drop her off.

"Okay since dad is dropping you off, I guess I'll you see you two tonight. Jasmine before I forget, invite the baby's father and his parent's over for dinner tonight. Your dad and I would like to meet them. Alright let me get out of here, before I'm late to work. Love you." "Come on Jasmine, we also need to go."

It was already hard enough for Jasmine to figure out whether she was going to have her baby, now she must explain to her parents that Dontrelle is no longer in the picture. During the entire ride to school all Jasmine could think about was how she was going to tell her parents who Dontrelle was to her and that he wanted nothing to do with her or their unborn child.

Regardless of the decision that Jasmine chooses to make concerning her pregnancy, and how she will tell her parents about her non-existing relationship with Dontrelle, it will have to wait until after school.

"Alright, madame princess, we have arrived at your requested destination and that will be ten dollars."

"Ha, ha dad...thank you and put it on my tab. Chauffeur, you can come back and pick me up from school around three-thirty."

"Get out of here girl so I won't be late to work. By the way, your mother will be picking you up from school because I have a parent-teacher conference this afternoon. Okay, kiddo love you and have a good day at school."

As soon as Jasmine exited her father's car she accidently bumped into Angel. "Dang girl! Watch where you walking." Without responding to Angel's comment, Jasmine ignored her and continued to walk toward the building where her locker was located.

As Jasmine approached her locker, she heard Angel call her name," Hey Jasmine." When she turned to see what Angel wanted, she mumbled under-breath to herself, "what does she want with me." "Yes, Angel what do you want?"

"First, I want an apology from you for bumping into me a minute ago. Secondly, I want to know why when I asked you months ago if you knew my boyfriend Dontrelle you didn't tell me that you had dated before."

After hearing what Angel had to say, Jasmine stood speechless for a second wondering how Angel found out that she had dated Dontrelle.

"Angel, I apologize for bumping into you earlier, I didn't see you as I was getting out of my dad's car. As for me dating Dontrelle, I knew nothing of you while I was with him. By the time I met you, he and I were no longer together."

"Well that doesn't excuse the fact that when I asked you if you knew him, you told me that the two of you were just friends. And now I find out that you are pregnant with his baby. What do you have to say about that?"

Shocked and embarrassed by what Angel had just disclosed in front of their classmates and some teachers, Jasmine dropped her books and ran crying to the girl's restroom. Observing the chaos that had occurred in the hallway between Jasmine and Angel, Mrs. Dennison, the language arts teacher, reported the incident to the counselor's office.

While Jasmine was in the restroom, trying to regain her composure, she heard her name called over the school's intercom. "Jasmine Sawman, please report immediately to the counselor's office." Unsure why she was being summoned to the counselor's office, Jasmine quickly dried her tears and proceeded to the office.

As Jasmine walked to the counselor's office, she noticed a group of girls who witnessed the altercation between her and Angel standing by the office door. When she opened the door, they began to point their fingers at her stomach and smirk at her.

Because she didn't want to bring any more attention to herself, Jasmine walked into the office without looking back. Before Jasmine could inform anyone in the counselor's office of who she was her name was again called over the intercom. "Jasmine Sawman please report immediately to the counselor's office."

When the secretary noticed Jasmine nervously standing at her desk she said, "You must be Jasmine Sawman?"

"Yes ma' am someone called for me to report to this office."

"Oh yes, that was me that called for you, Mrs. Turner, your guidance counselor, would like to speak with you. Have a seat and she will be with you in a minute."

After waiting for nearly five minutes Mrs. Turner appeared and escorted Jasmine to her office. "Hello Jasmine, I'm Mrs. Turner and I called you to my office because it has been reported to me that you had a verbal altercation this morning with another student by the name of Angel Fletcher. During this argument it was revealed that you may be pregnant. As you well know, according to St. Catherine's student code of conduct, girls who are discovered to be pregnant are no longer allowed to attend our school. Therefore, I wanted to speak with you in private to get your version of the story and to find out if this is true or not before this incident was reported to the headmistress of the school and your parents."

Jasmine slowly responded, "Yes, there was a verbal altercation between me and Angel, but she started with me. And no disrespect Mrs. Turner but when it comes to asking me questions about my health, my parents will need to be present."

Once Mrs. Turner realized that Jasmine was no longer going to speak with her, she informed Jasmine that she had no choice but to report the matter to the headmistress and schedule a conference with her parents.

"Okay Jasmine, I guess I will continue this conversation with you and your parents tomorrow when we meet for our conference. You can go now. Make sure you get a pass to class."

For the rest of the school day Jasmine kept to herself and avoided interaction with Angel and other classmates. When school was finally over Jasmine quickly went to the designated area for car riders and waited for her mother to pick her up.

While Jasmine stood waiting for her mother, Angel approached her and tried to start an argument with her about her relationship with Dontrelle and the fact that she was pregnant with his child. However, before an argument could ensue Peggy arrived. "Jasmine, Jasmine, come on we gotta go."

At the same time Jasmine was getting into the car, her mother began to tell her that she received a phone call from the counseling office to schedule an appointment for the next day because the school had information that Jasmine could be pregnant.

When Jasmine informed her mother of how the school found out that she could be pregnant, Peggy became enraged and said that she was going to have a talk with the school to let them know that they needed to first speak with parents when they receive information of that nature and not take the word of a child.

Seeing how upset her mother got, Jasmine asked to be withdrawn from St. Catherine's Academy and sent back to Mountain View High so that she could avoid the expulsion process. That way no one would know if it was true that she was pregnant.

Jasmine went on to explain to her mother that she and the father of her unborn child were no longer together, that he wanted her to get an abortion and that the girl who outed her at school was also pregnant with his child. Not believing what Jasmine was saying, Peggy told her that they would continue the conversation at home when her father got in from work.

By the time Carl arrived home Jasmine had fallen asleep. While Jasmine's parents waited for her to wake up from her nap, they discussed how they were going to contact Dontrelle and his parents regarding their daughter being pregnant with his child.

Amid the Sawmans discussing the issue of their daughter's pregnancy, Jasmine frantically entered the room where her parents were sitting and informed them that she needed to go to the hospital because she woke up and her bed was full of blood.

Upon arriving at the hospital and being evaluated by medical staff it was determined that Jasmine had a miscarriage due to unforeseen stress that she had experienced from the time she found out that she was pregnant. When the doctors informed Peggy and Carl that Jasmine had lost their grandchild, they embraced one another and simultaneously said, "I can't believe this is happening to our baby girl."

After the Sawmans hugged one another they realized that they had to set aside their feelings of sadness, so they could be emotionally available for Jasmine while she transitioned through the stages of grieving. Carl and Peggy tried their best to remain supportive of their daughter, however, when Jasmine was released from the hospital and returned to school, she fell into a deep depression and spent the next several weeks crying and being angry with everyone she encountered.

Feeling helpless and not knowing how to help Jasmine cope with the loss of her baby, Peggy decided to call on one of the prayer warriors in her church, Sandra Buckman, to ask her to intercede in prayer on behalf of Jasmine. While the two ladies were talking, Peggy asked Sandra how her son Charles was doing and thought since he and Jasmine had been longtime childhood friends it would be a good idea if he could stop by their house to possibly cheer her up.

Although Sandra thought it was a good idea for her son to visit Jasmine, she believed it was too soon, and instead suggested that Peggy get Jasmine some counseling. Not keen on counseling, Peggy reluctantly thanked Sandra and told her that she would speak with her on a later date. Peggy felt so desperate that she reached out to Sheila to see if she could help uplift Jasmine's spirit. Even that did not help.

As time progressed Carl and Peggy noticed that Jasmine's depression got worse; she had difficulty sleeping, eating and concentrating on her schoolwork. Because Jasmine had so much trouble dealing with everyday tasks, her parents decided to get her some counseling.

Carl and Peggy also decided that Jasmine would no longer attend school at St. Catherine's Academy nor would she reenroll at Mountain View High. Jasmine would instead complete the rest of her high school education taking online courses through a home-school based program.

Despite Jasmine getting pregnant at an early age and miscarrying, spending three and a half years in counseling, not being able to complete her high school education in a traditional school setting, Jasmine managed to regain normalcy as a teenager. Jasmine did so well at the latter part of her high school matriculation, she graduated from the homeschool program with a 3.5 grade point average and obtained an academic scholarship to attend college at Central A & M University in Tallahassee, Florida, where she planned to study business and marketing.

The next chapter of Jasmine's life would be challenging, but it would prove to be a vital part in the further development of her character as a young woman, someone who was seeking to find their self-worth and value in life.

TWISTED LOVE

Somethings that Seem to be Good May Actually be Danger Wrapped up in a Flattering Package

CHAPTER 9

The day Jasmine had dreamed about for months had finally come. She was preparing to leave for college to embark on a new journey in life. Jasmine's enthusiasm, however, was not shared by her parents. Carl and Peggy were not quite enthusiastic as Jasmine, they were concerned that their youngest child, who experienced the loss of her child and had an emotional breakdown, would again experience the same thing, if not worse. The Sawmans did not waste any time expressing how they felt about Jasmine going to school so far away from home while at the same time losing her support system.

"Jasmine, can you come in the living room? Your father and I would like to speak with you before we hit the road to Florida."

While Carl and Peggy waited downstairs for Jasmine to join them in the living room, Carl reminded his wife that they didn't have much time to speak to their daughter about her attending Central A & M University. Carl insisted that he and his wife keep the conversation with Jasmine down to ten minutes because they needed to get on the road.

"Yes, mom and dad. What did you want to talk about?"

"Jasmine before we leave, your father and I would like to know why you chose to go to CAMU?"

"Mom, just before it's time for us to leave, you want to ask me this. It should be obvious to the both of you why I chose to attend CAMU, they offered me a full academic scholarship. Isn't that what you have always expected from Ashley, Allison, and me? To be able to attend college for free? No disrespect mom and dad, but what is the real reason you waited until now to ask me this ridiculous question?"

"Jasmine, your mother and I just want to be reassured that you will be okay while you are away at school because you won't be near family."

Amid Carl speaking, Peggy chimed in, "Yes Jazz you've been through a lot over the last few years."

"I realize that I won't be around family. I also have not forgotten what I've been through these past three and a half years. I believe attending Central A & M University will be good for me because it will give me a new outlook on life, I will be in a new environment and I will have the opportunity to meet different people. Mom and dad, it's time that you trust me, I'm not depressed anymore. Anyway, I won't be alone because last week I found out that Sheila will be going to CAMU as well."

Discovering that Sheila would be attending CAMU with Jasmine, Carl and Peggy felt more accepting of their daughter's college choice and proceeded to apologize for thinking that she was not capable enough to make a wise decision on her own. Jasmine accepted her parent's apology and reminded them it was getting late and they still needed to pack their van for the trip. Once the Sawman's van was packed, they prayed and asked God to bless their trip to Florida.

Throughout the entire trip to Tallahassee no one spoke a word until Jasmine saw a road sign that read *Welcome to Florida* and she yelled out loud, "Yay we are almost there, mom and dad!"

With tears in their eyes, Carl and Peggy glanced over at each other and realized they had to embrace their new norm in life; their youngest child was now a college freshman and they were empty-nesters. Nevertheless, shortly after seeing the welcome to Florida sign Carl, Peggy and Jasmine arrived on the campus of Central A & M University. As soon as they arrived on campus, they were instructed by campus police to go directly to the gymnasium to complete freshman check-in. After Jasmine completed her check-in paperwork and obtained her dormitory key, she and her parents drove around the campus until they found her dorm.

When Carl found a parking spot and parked, Jasmine proceeded to get out. Immediately she noticed a young man at a car a few spaces over from her family's van unloading and carrying his belongings into the building adjacent to her dorm. Noticing her daughter was staring at the young man, Peggy snapped her fingers in front of Jasmine's face and said, "earth to Jasmine who are you looking at?"

"Oh, huh nothing mom, let's unpack the van so you and dad can get back on the road."

It took Jasmine and her parent's less than an hour and a half to move-in and set up her dorm room. As soon as Jasmine's room was completed, Carl and Peggy decided to take her out for dinner before they left to return home in Swainsboro, Georgia.

After Jasmine and her parents had dinner, they returned to the campus of CAMU. Taking into consideration that it was getting late, Carl and Peggy cut their good-byes short and wished her a successful school year. When Peggy hugged Jasmine she immediately began to cry. Hearing her mother cry again Jasmine said, "Mom you are crying again?"

"Jasmine, I'm not just crying because I'm going to miss you. I'm crying because I'm so proud of the young woman you have become and the fact you didn't let what you went through in the past stop you from pursuing your goals."

Carl and Peggy both hugged Jasmine at the same time and again said, "We are going to miss you Jazz!"

"Oh, dad and mom you'll act like I'm never going to come home to visit you guys on the weekends and holiday breaks. Don't forget that Swainsboro is only an hour and a half away from Tallahassee. So, stop crying and worrying I'm going to be okay."

Feeling reassured and a sense of relief by Jasmine's "farewell," Carl and Peggy prayed a prayer of protection over their daughter and asked God to grant them travelling grace for their journey home. After they prayed, they hugged Jasmine one last time then left to go back home. While Jasmine stood in the parking lot of her dorm waving bye to her parents, the young man she saw earlier during the day approached her, and said, "What's up, I see your parents are leaving." "Excuse me?", Jasmine responded.

"I'm sorry if I scared you. I'm Isaac. How are you doing? I was just saying bye to my parents and noticed you were saying bye to your parents as well. So, I thought I would come over to introduce myself."

Not trying to give away that she noticed him from earlier, Jasmine quickly replied, "Hi,

I'm Jasmine. I didn't mean to sound so rude when you came up to me, but it is dark out here and you can't be too careful with people you don't know."

"I completely understand. Jasmine if I may ask, where are you from?", Isaac inquired.

"I am from a small town in Georgia called Swainsboro. Where are you from?"

"Cleveland, Ohio," Isaac answered.

After talking for nearly an hour and going back and forth asking each other questions, Jasmine told Isaac that she was tired and needed to prepare for bed. Before Jasmine walked away from where she and Isaac were standing, he asked her if it would be okay if they saw each other the next day and she agreed. "When you come tomorrow, tell the person at the front desk that you would like to see Jasmine Sawman in room 309." Jasmine and Isaac wished each other a good night and retreated to their new home away from home.

Once Jasmine said good night to Isaac and begin to walk toward her dorm, she received a call from Sheila," Hey girl, where you at?"

"Walking back toward my dorm," Jasmine responded.

"And what dorm is that?", Sheila asked.
"Wheats Hall."

"Oh, snap that's the dorm I'm in. What floor?"

"I'm on the third floor in room 309," Jasmine answered.

"Wow, that's crazy I'm on the same floor in room 314. Since you are headed back to your room, stop by my room and help me finish unpacking."

"Uh, okay but I'm not going to stay that long because I'm tired. See you in a minute."

In less than five minutes Jasmine arrived at Sheila's room. As soon as Sheila opened her room door to let Jasmine in, they both begin to scream and hug one another. "Hey, Sheila it's so good to see you. By the way how did you end up coming to CAMU?", Jasmine asked.

"Girl, I had to escape the craziness of my family, plus I was offered a basketball scholarship."

"And when did you start playing basketball?", Jasmine inquired.

"I joined the basketball team shortly after you left Mountain View High to help deal with the stress I was experiencing at home.

Jasmine, so much has happened in my life since the last time you and I spoke."

"Why didn't you call me? I could have been there for you."

"Seriously Jasmine, you had your own problems you were dealing with at the time. Nevertheless, I believe my life up to this point has turned out just the way it was supposed to. Just think, had I not gone through what I went through at home, I would not be sitting here, at college, talking to you."

"Okay then, well said. I'm glad your life turned out this way for you, now we can travel this new road in life together, as best friends should." As the night progressed, Jasmine and Sheila continued talking about the things that happened to them over the past few years.

The next day came and as promised, Isaac returned to Jasmine's dorm to visit her, however, she was unavailable to receive visitors because she was asleep. After discovering that Jasmine was still asleep, Isaac decided to leave a message to inform her that he came by to see her.

Once Jasmine woke up, she got dressed and decided to go to the cafeteria to get something to eat before breakfast ended. On her way to the cafeteria Jasmine stopped by

Sheila's room to see if she wanted to go with her to catch a late breakfast, but Sheila was still asleep.

As Jasmine was walking to the cafeteria for breakfast she bumped into Isaac. "Hi, Jasmine where are you headed?"

"Good morning Isaac, I'm headed to the cafeteria to eat breakfast before it's too late."

"Cool, do you mind if I tag along with you? Also, did you get my message, that I stopped by this morning to see you?", he asked.

"Sure, I don't mind and no I didn't receive your message." As Jasmine and Isaac settled down in the cafeteria, Isaac asked Jasmine if she had a boyfriend back at home.

"Well, aren't you bold. Being that we just met yesterday, you want to know a lot about me."

"Jasmine, you seem like a person I would like to get to know a little better. I just don't want to waste my time getting to know you if you are not interested in me."

"That's fair enough," Jasmine replied. The conversation between Jasmine and Isaac continued until cafeteria staff said that breakfast was over.

While escorting Jasmine to her dorm, Isaac told her that he liked her and wanted to know if it would be okay if they spent more time together. He also informed her that at times it would be difficult to see her because he was on the football team. Jasmine felt so flattered by Isaac's straightforwardness and honesty, she said yes.

Unfortunately, as Jasmine and Isaac's relationship developed, he became possessive of her. Isaac began to require that she call or text him every day before and after class as well as before she went to bed. Isaac's controlling and neurotic behavior reached a point that his treatment of her affected her course work, grades, and social life.

Beyond Jasmine's relationship with Isaac impacting her college life, it began to change the way she communicated with her parents and friends. Isaac had gone as far as to monitor Jasmine's calls to her parents. Jasmine could only call her parents if Isaac was present.

One day, while Jasmine was visiting Sheila in her room, Sheila asked her, "Jasmine is everything alright with you?" "Yes, everything is alright with me. Why?"

"I ask because things with you have gotten weird. Every time I call to see if you want to hang out with me, you tell me you can't. Are you seeing somebody?" "Matter of fact, I am."

"Well that explains why you are always busy when I call you." "Now that you know I'm dating someone, are you going to become that annoying big sister friend like back in high school when I dated Dontrelle?" "Yes, I will if you start acting strange!"

"No worries Sheila. Everything is good with me. Better yet it's great. I think this guy is the one. Anyway, you my girl, if anything should go wrong in my relationship with my new boo, you'll be the first person I tell."

"Okay, if you say so. I just don't want you to end up like you did when everything with Dontrelle ended. Can I meet this mysterious boyfriend today?"

"No, not today but you will meet him soon."

"There must be something wrong with this dude and that's why you don't want me to meet him today."

"There you go again, with your conspiracy theories, and being that overly protective friend."

"That's not it at all, I just don't want anything bad to happen to my best friend!"

"Girl, nothing bad is going to happen to me. Now if you are done interrogating me about my love life, let's go to the Green Room to get something to eat because I'm hungry."

Despite Jasmine sharing with Sheila about her new relationship with Isaac, Sheila has no clue that all the fluff that Jasmine has sold her is nothing but a lie. The truth is, Jasmine has been suffering emotional, verbal, and physical abuse at the hands of Isaac. She accepts this treatment because he is someone she truly cares for and believes she can help change.

CHAPTER 10

Over the next several years the abuse that Jasmine endures at the hand of Isaac intensifies. One day, while on his way to football practice, Isaac noticed Jasmine sitting in the library. When Isaac went in the library to say hello to Jasmine, he discovered that she was sitting at a table accompanied by mostly male students. Seeing Jasmine surrounded by so many men caused Isaac's jealously to get the best of him. He caused a scene in the atrium of the library.

"Jasmine, I thought you told me earlier that you were meeting friends to study for your Global Marketing class but instead I find you sitting here with these punks!"

"Isaac, if you calm down, I will explain who they are."

"No, I don't want to hear what you have to say."

Feeling embarrassed by Isaac's behavior, Jasmine apologized to her classmates and told them that she would call them later to reschedule another study group. As Jasmine turned to leave, Isaac suddenly grabbed her by the waist and began twisting it saying, "come on let's go." The librarian who witnessed the incident between Isaac and Jasmine notified the campus police. Before Isaac and Jasmine could exit the building, the police arrived.

When the officers entered the library, they immediately separated Isaac and Jasmine. One of the policemen, Officer Bello, pulled Isaac to the side and requested to see his student ID. Meanwhile, Officer McKenzie questioned Jasmine about what happened with Isaac.

"Hello young lady is everything okay with you? We received a call from the library stating that a person with the same description of the young man standing with my partner was pulling a young woman against her will. Were you the young woman we received the call about?"

"Yes, I'm that young lady and to answer your second question, I'm okay officer." "Do you wish to press charges?", Officer McKenzie asked.

"No, I do not wish to press charges against him. He's my boyfriend and we just had a misunderstanding, that's all."

"Do you know how many times over the last fifteen years of being a police officer I've heard that statement come from young women such as yourself? Now I can't tell you what to do but I would like to offer you some advice if you should ever need help or support leaving your boyfriend, please seek the aide of the campus abuse hotline. With that being said, since you do not want to press charges, we are done here." Before Officer McKenzie walked away from Jasmine, she told her to take care of herself and to seek help if she needed it.

Because of the campus police being called to investigate the confrontation in the library, Isaac took his frustration of being questioned by the police and missing football practice out on Jasmine. Isaac was so enraged that as he drove Jasmine back to her apartment he repeatedly punched her and yelled obscenities at her. Isaac punched Jasmine so hard that the entire left side of her face was bruised.

After Isaac and Jasmine arrived at her home, he threatened her, telling her that if she told anyone what happened to her, he would do it again, but the next time, things would get worst. Once Jasmine realized that Isaac's threat was serious, she spent the next several days telling her friends and professors that she obtained her injuries from falling down a flight of stairs at her apartment complex.

There was one person in Jasmine's life, however, that didn't believe her story and that person was Sheila. One day, while talking on the telephone with Sheila, Jasmine let it slip out that Isaac had punched her in the mouth. Jasmine excused his action by saying it was an accident and he didn't mean to do it.

"How long has that nut been hitting on you?", Sheila asked.

"Sheila don't call him a nut, he does have a name."

"This dude beating up on you and you have the nerve to correct me on what name I should call him? Jasmine, you remind me of my mother. She used to always make excuses and defend my father after he got drunk and knocked her around. Honestly, I don't get women like you or my mother; neither one of you were raised in an abusive household but you allow a man, who claims to love you, to put his hands on you. Why stay with a person who's not going to change? As the old saying goes, leopards don't change their spots."

"Sheila are you done? Do you mind if I speak?" "Go ahead, I'm done."

"Okay, first please don't be offended by what I'm about to say, but my relationship with Isaac is none of your business. I know I let it slip by telling you what Isaac did to me but now you know I don't need your judgement or criticism. For once in our relationship as friends, Sheila, can you just be there for me and not offer any advice?"

"Jasmine, you are one of my closest friends and I love you. Please consider leaving Isaac before he does something to you, like kill you."

"Sheila nothing like that is going to happen to me. Isaac won't risk losing his football scholarship and the possibility of going to jail. Besides I think with a little love, prayer and understanding I can help him change into a better person."

"Jasmine, I don't mean any disrespect, but you can't change anyone, not even yourself. Furthermore, coming from someone who grew-up in a household where abuse was the norm, nothing is going to get any better between you and Isaac."

"Well, Sheila I hear you loud and clear and I'll try to take what you said into consideration. Sheila, before we hang-up, I need you to promise me that you will not tell anyone what we talked about tonight."

"If that's what you want, cool. But I want you to know this Jasmine if I see your life being threatened, I will notify your parents and law enforcement."

"Thanks girl and don't worry about me. Everything is going to be alright between Isaac and me, you'll see."

"Um, hm. I'll talk to you later. Call me if you need anything."

Seemingly things between Jasmine and Isaac got better. For a short period of time Isaac treated Jasmine like a queen. On several occasions Isaac would show up to Jasmine's apartment and surprise her with a dozen roses, chocolate candies and love letters attached to stuff animals. It would seem like Jasmine was correct when she suggested to Sheila that love, prayer, and understanding could help change Isaac.

However, Jasmine's philosophy on the treatment of her abuser was wrong. Jasmine and Isaac's relationship took a sudden turn for the worst when he received news that he didn't make the cut to be team captain of the football team for the upcoming football season, his senior season. Feeling like a failure, Isaac soon takes his frustration out on Jasmine.

The relationship between Jasmine and Isaac becomes so tumultuous that Jasmine again falls victim to Isaac's fist and foot. One day Isaac beat Jasmine to the point that she sustained a concussion, two broken ribs, a busted eye and a fractured jaw. Jasmine's injuries were so severe that she was admitted to the hospital.

When staff from the hospital's admission office asked Jasmine who she wanted them to contact on her behalf, she thought about it before she gave a response. As Jasmine pondered if she should have the hospital to contact her parents or Sheila, she decided not to have them to contact anyone. Jasmine did not want to contact her parents because she knew they would worry and make her come home.

Likewise, she didn't want the hospital to contact Sheila because she would have to admit to her that she was right about Isaac not changing. Ten minutes lapsed before Jasmine gave the hospital admission rep an answer. Since Jasmine was unable to speak, she elected to write out her response to the hospital admission staff on a piece of paper. Jasmine's written response read: *There's no one I wish for you to contact on my behalf.*

Because of Jasmine's decision to not inform anyone of her injuries, she spends the next two months recovering in silence. Jasmine decided, out of guilt and shame, to never divulge to anyone what she endured at the hands of her lover, Isaac. Ironically, Isaac was never arrested for assaulting Jasmine simply because she refused to disclose to the police how she sustained her injuries.

Jasmine's choice to heal in seclusion leads her to spend time completing class assignments as well as reflecting on what she wanted her life to look like after college. Fortunately, Jasmine's plans did not include Isaac.

Jasmine finally concluded that she had spent most of her time in college catering to a man who did nothing but abuse her. Coming to this revelation, Jasmine decided that it was time to end her relationship with Isaac.

Instead of meeting Isaac face to face, Jasmine wrote him a letter expressing her feelings and explaining why she chose to end their relationship.

CHAPTER 11

In the five months since Jasmine ended her relationship with Isaac, it appeared that her outlook on life improved. Jasmine's closest friends had also noticed that she changed for the better. With her newfound freedom, Jasmine realized that she never got to truly experience the fullness of college life because from the time her parents dropped her off at school, she had spent every waking moment with Isaac. Jasmine's joyful disposition and outgoing attitude resulted in her becoming a socialite on the campus of CAMU.

Over the span of a semester Jasmine joins various organizations. She becomes an avid member of CAMU's community outreach program, the BusMark Association and the

Zorga Foundation, a mentoring program for foster children who have aged out of the system but want to attend college. Jasmine also finds herself, after three years of hiatus, going back to church and volunteering with the CAMU's campus ministry. It appears that Jasmine has finally recovered from the years of her involvement with Isaac.

However, Jasmine's distant past with Isaac resurfaces when she received news, from Sheila, that Isaac had been placed on academic probation because he was arrested for assaulting and raping his new girlfriend. It was at that moment that Jasmine realized that the life she had been living for the past few months was all a lie.

Jasmine began to feel a sense of guilt and shame all over again. She thought to herself that if she would have reported the beating incident to the police the previous school term, Isaac would have never had a chance to abuse another person.

After discovering that Isaac victimized another student, Jasmine decided it was time to tell her story. As not to reveal her identity, Jasmine sent an anonymous letter to CAMU's Student Peer Review Council describing how Isaac would abuse her and suggested that the school revise its policy on the reporting of abuse and assault on campus.

Furthermore, Jasmine stated that changes to the school's abuse policy would encourage more reporting of campus abuse among students. Feeling liberated by sharing what she endured, Jasmine pressed through to complete her senior year of college.

Nevertheless, Jasmine's last year attending Central A & M University ended on an epic note. She graduated at the top of her class receiving a Bachelor's in Business & Marketing with a minor in Finance. With a recommendation from the department chair of her program, Jasmine successfully landed an entry-level position at the Centél Firm in Atlanta, Georgia.

Although Jasmine's next journey in adulthood would begin in a new city it will include a familiar face, her longtime friend, Sheila. Sheila had also graduated from college and she had secured a teaching position with a school district in the greater Atlanta area. What new exciting adventures and opportunities await these two young ladies in the urban corridor of the "Big Apple" of the south?

THE LUST FACTOR

Lust Reveals Selfish Intent

CHAPTER 12

Since graduating and relocating to the Atlanta area, Jasmine and Sheila successfully settled into their new apartment and started their new careers. They also managed to meet new people and go out on dates. Things were so good for Jasmine at work that she had caught the attention of Curtis Brockton, team leader for the marketing division at the Centél Firm.

Noticing how smart and talented Jasmine was, Curtis risked his status and career at the Centél Firm to ask her out for dinner. Jasmine tried her best to ignore his advances because she realized that fraternizing with her supervisor could be detrimental to her career and future at the Centél Firm. After several attempts to convince Jasmine to go to dinner with him, Jasmine finally gave in and agreed to go out with him. Regrettably, Jasmine had no clue that Curtis was a married man with two children.

Over the next several months Jasmine and Curtis secretly spend time getting to know one another intimately. Most of Jasmine and Curtis' time with each other is spent going to dinner, the movies, hanging out at her apartment with Sheila and her boyfriend James, taking mini staycations at local bed and breakfast resorts and traveling to Swainsboro to visit her parents.

As time went by, Jasmine realized that she had fallen deeply in love with Curtis. She believed it was time for their relationship to be made public. However, Curtis did not share the same sentiment.

One day, while having dinner at their usual meet up spot, Le Chez Capri, Curtis expressed his concerns to Jasmine why it was not the right time to make their relationship known to everyone.

"Hey Jasmine thanks for meeting me tonight."

"Oh, Curtis you don't have to thank me, you know this is our night to meet for dinner."

"I know but I wanted to let you know how thankful I am for you being in my life. Jasmine before our waiter comes to take our order, I have somethings I need to discuss with you."

"What is it that you need to talk to me about?"

"Well earlier this week you mentioned that you wanted to make our relationship public, but I don't think it would be wise to do that. Jasmine, do you know that if word gets back to Human Resource at Centél both of our careers will be destroyed?"

"I realize that Curtis but I'm tired of sneaking around. It feels like I'm the other woman that must remain a secret."

"That's not it at all. I'm just looking out for our careers."

"Okay, I understand that now is not the time to tell anyone about us, but I don't want to spend the rest of our relationship running around, pretending like we are not dating."

"Alright got it, now that that matter has been settled let's order because I'm starving."

While Curtis and Jasmine waited for their food to arrive, Monica Mathis, a member of their team from work so happen to walk pass the window of Le Chez Capri and noticed them laughing, holding hands, and playing footsie underneath the table. Unaware that they had been spotted, Jasmine and Curtis continued to enjoy their evening together. The very next day at work Jasmine was confronted by Monica.

"Good morning Jasmine and how are you on this beautiful work day?"

Jasmine hesitatingly responded, "Good morning Monica, everything is okay, I think."

"Jasmine, why does it sound like you don't believe I'm being sincere when I ask you how your day is going?"

"Maybe because outside of completing our work assignments you don't talk to me."

"Well, Jasmine, I just stopped by your desk to tell you that last night I saw you and Mr. Brockton at Le Chez Capri's holding hands. It seems like you both were having a good time together. I'm not trying to get into your personal business, but you better watch yourself with that man."

"What do you mean, I should watch myself with Mr. Brockton?"

"I mean watch yourself. Mr. Brockton has a representation of seducing the new and inexperienced workers around the office."

"Not to be rude or anything, but how do you know?"

"I know what he is capable of because it happened to me five years ago, when I started working on his team."

"What happened? Why did your relationship with him end?"

"It's complicated and I don't want to get into that right now. Just watch yourself because dealing with Mr. Brockton is like playing with fire, sooner or later you will get burned."

As the conversation between Jasmine and Monica ended, Jasmine stood perplexed, wondering to herself what did Monica mean when she stated that being involved with Curtis was like *"dealing with fire."* Jasmine spent the rest of her work day fighting off the thoughts that were plaguing her mind from the conversation with Monica. Nonetheless, Jasmine would soon discover the true meaning behind Monica's statement about their boss.

CHAPTER 13

Several days had passed since the conversation between Jasmine and Monica took place. Unknowingly to them, Linda Cooper, a former team member of Curtis Brockton, overheard the two ladies' conversation and decided it was time to report to upper-level management and the HR Department of Centél everything she knew about Curtis' sexual advances toward female employees assigned to his team.

Within a matter of days of Linda reporting Curtis to Centél's HR Department, Jasmine's fairytale relationship with him quickly went from daisies in the park to a nightmare on a deserted island. Because of the investigation that ensued after allegations were brought to the attention of upper management by Linda, Curtis was placed on administrative leave until the probe into his behavior was completed.

The assertions made by Linda Cooper about Curtis' behavior were proven to be true. Based on the findings of the investigation into Curtis' behavior, it was revealed that Jasmine and Monica were not the first two female employees to fall prey to his seductive behavior. It was also revealed that Curtis' behavior of fraternizing with female employees spanned over ten years. Hence, due to the damaging information that the human resource department received about Curtis' behavior, it was recommended that he be terminated immediately from the Centél Firm.

Additionally, Curtis' wife, Regina Brockton, Centél's Communication Division Supervisor, was also under scrutiny throughout the investigation process because she had knowledge of her husband's behavior. It was later deemed that Regina was complicit in her husband's behavior because she knew for years that he had a habit of preying on female subordinates but did nothing to report it or stop it. Due to her failure to report her husband, Regina was also released from her duties with the Centél Firm.

Nevertheless, shortly after learning that he had been terminated from his position with the Centél Firm, Curtis returned to his former office to retrieve his personal belongings. Observing that someone was in Curtis' office, Jasmine decided to find out what was going on and to her surprise it was Curtis removing his things.

As to not give away that she was romantically involved with Curtis, Jasmine addressed him professionally, "Hi Mr. Brockton, welcome back! If I'm not being too intrusive where have you been the last few days?" However, Curtis ignored Jasmine by remaining silent because it struck him that she might have had something to do with his termination, but his assumptions were wrong.

"Jasmine, I think it would be best if you would leave this office now."

"I haven't you seen in days and this is how you talk to me. What's your problem?"

"I don't have a problem, I just don't feel like being bothered."

Curtis paused for a second and then said, "You know what, I do have a problem.

I've been fired, and I believe you had something to with it."

"What are you talking about, I didn't even know you were fired until just now when you told me."

"Jasmine, it doesn't matter what you say or how innocent you try to portray yourself, I know you sabotaged my career. I suspect you did it all because you wanted more in this so-called relationship than I was willing to give you."

Feeling adamant about his claim, Curtis again insisted that Jasmine leave his office so that he could finish packing his belongings. At Curtis' request Jasmine turned to exit the office but before she could leave, she spotted a picture of Curtis standing with a woman and two children.

After seeing the picture Jasmine blurted out loud, "Curtis, before I leave this office explain to me who you are standing with in this picture?"

"It's my wife and two sons. Now if that answers your question, please leave my office."

As Jasmine exited Curtis' office she sarcastically replied, "It's not your office anymore, you were fired remember," and slammed the door.

A flood of emotions overtook Jasmine as she ran off to the restroom to cry. From the news that Curtis was a married man with children, Jasmine realized why she never met any of his family or friends, why they always had to meet at secret locations, or go to late night movies. Jasmine finally understood that her entire relationship with Curtis was a sham and everything she thought she knew about him had all been a lie.

CHAPTER 14

From the time Jasmine found out that Curtis was married with two children, she spent the next three months despondent. At work Jasmine communicated with her co-workers just enough to get assignments completed. Meanwhile, at home, Jasmine reframed from talking because she feared that Sheila would chastise her again for picking another loser boyfriend. One day, while Jasmine and Sheila were meal prepping, Sheila asked Jasmine what was wrong with her and why she wouldn't talk to her.

"Sheila there's nothing wrong with me. I just don't feel like talking to anyone."

"Jasmine, I can understand that you may not want to talk to anyone, I get into those types of funks but not for three months. There's something seriously wrong with you."

"As I stated before, there's nothing wrong with me. I wish you would just mind your own business."

"Okay, if that's how you feel I won't say anything to you again."

Suddenly and out of no way Jasmine began to cry. Believing she was right about something bothering Jasmine, Sheila decided not to respond in her normal manner but instead embrace Jasmine.

"Jasmine I know you don't want to tell me what's bothering you but whatever it is you need to tell someone. Don't let this destroy you emotionally."

Realizing that Sheila was right, Jasmine took a deep breath and revealed to her the issue that had bothered her the last few months. "Well do you remember Curtis from my job?"

"Yes, I remember him. That's the guy you would invite over to hang out with us. What about him?"

"He's the reason why I've been moping around for the last several months. I found out that he only dated me for sex. And that's not the worse part. I also discovered that he had a habit of dating all the young new female employees that were assigned to his team and he was married with two kids."

"Wow, that's a lot to deal with. I see why you didn't want to talk to anyone. So tell me, what are you going to do about him?" "Nothing." "Why not, you need to report him to human resource and get him fired," Sheila stated.

"No need, he's already been fired and as far as the situation with Curtis being married, I'm not going to worry about that because he'll get what's coming to him. You know what *they* say about karma. I'm going to allow this moment to be another lesson learned."

"Ahh, Jasmine I am so proud of you, continue to keep that positive vibe. I know one day God will send you Mr. Right."

For the first time in a long time Jasmine and Sheila spent the evening talking and reminiscing about the things they experienced together since they met in high school.

TWO FACES OF FRENEMIES

*The True Essence of a Person Will
Always Show Itself*

CHAPTER 15

After several years of being involved with the wrong man and working at the Centél Firm, Jasmine decided it was time to redirect her focus in life onto her personal growth and professional development. However, her stance to remain single and advance her career within the marketing industry would soon be challenged. One day while at work Jasmine shared with her co-worker, Rhoda, that she wanted to broaden her social connections.

During their conversation Rhoda informed Jasmine about an upcoming Atlanta Networking Mixer for young professionals and thought that it would benefit her if she attended. Since it would be her first time attending the mixer and she would not know anyone at the event, Jasmine asked Sheila if she wouldn't mind tagging along.

The day of the networking event had come, and Jasmine and Sheila were excited to attend. When they arrived at the event they were impressed by the number of young professionals that were in attendance, especially the male attendees. Throughout the entire evening Jasmine and Sheila spent their time mingling with different sets of people. Ironically, Jasmine spent most of her time conversing with Reggie Haynes, a corporate executive at SoftMax Technology.

While Sheila was talking to a colleague from work, who also was attending the mixer, she noticed from across the room that Jasmine was in deep conversation with a handsome man. Being the curious person that she is, Sheila excused herself from the conversation with her coworker and walked over to where Jasmine and the gentleman were standing, interjecting herself into their conversation.

"Hola, handsome and what is your name?"

"Hello, I think, I'm Reggie and you are?"

"Hi Reggie, I'm Sheila and this young lady you've been talking to all night is my best friend Jasmine. Reggie do you like her?"

Seeing that Sheila was a bit tipsy, Jasmine asked Reggie to excuse her so that she could take her friend home. But before Jasmine could leave, Reggie asked for her telephone number. However, Jasmine's immediate response to Reggie's request was, "I must decline because I'm not interested in dating anyone right now."

"No offense Jasmine, but I'm not trying to date you. I just want to continue our conversation. You had some interesting thoughts on global marketing, and I would like to hear more about it."

"Listen Reggie I apologize, I didn't mean to insinuate that you were trying to get with me. I would love to continue our discussion."

"Okay, enough with the back and forth you're making me sick. Ugh, I think I'm going to throw-up," Sheila said.

"Reggie can you please excuse me I need to get my friend home. Oh, before I forget here's my phone number."

As Jasmine proceeded to leave the mixer with Sheila, Reggie reminded her that he was going to call her the following day. The next day came and Reggie called Jasmine as he promised. The conversation between Jasmine and Reggie shifted suddenly, instead of discussing global marketing they talked about various topics such as their personal lives, professional goals, politics and places they have visited and wanted to visit.

Over time Jasmine and Reggie spent more and more time getting to know each other as friends. One day while on the phone with Reggie, Jasmine expressed how much she enjoyed talking to him.

"Reggie, I don't know if I have told you or not, but it is so refreshing to be able to hold a conversation with someone that has the same interests, I never thought I would ever meet someone like you."

"Wait a minute Jasmine, I think you're getting the wrong impression about our friendship. Do you remember when we first met, you informed me that you were not interested in dating anyone? Well, if truth be told neither am I. At this point in my life I'm not interested in seriously dating anyone."

"That's understandable, my apologies if I made you feel awkward by what I said.

Reggie, I did mean what I said, I do enjoy talking to you as a friend."

After several weeks of getting to know one another over the telephone and going on occasional dates, Jasmine begins to secretly form romantic feelings for Reggie. On the contrary, Reggie has also formed feelings for Jasmine but due to his stance on non-exclusive dating and womanizing ways, Jasmine will never know.

The friendship between Jasmine and Reggie evolves into one that closely resembles that of girlfriend and boyfriend. However, an outside entity will pose a threat to the further development of this relationship.

CHAPTER 16

Two years into their "friendship," Jasmine and Reggie have dated on and off. Throughout this time Jasmine and Reggie's relationship has been plagued with a series of lies and infidelity. The relationship that Jasmine has with Reggie bears an uncanny resemblance to a leech sucking the life out of its host.

One day, feeling a bit frustrated and overwhelmed by Reggie's womanizing antics and failure to commit to her, Jasmine decided that it was time that she gave him an ultimatum. When Jasmine gained the courage to express her feelings and present her demands to Reggie, things did not go as she had planned. The moment Jasmine told Reggie how she felt about their relationship, the conversation quickly turned into an argument.

"Look Jasmine. I told you from the jump that I didn't want to exclusively date one person. So, don't blame me because you chose to fall for me."

"Reggie don't flatter yourself! And trust me when I say that you would have been the last man I would have chosen. Answer this question, if you say you don't want to be with just one person, why is it that every time we stop seeing each other, you somehow find your way back in my life? Reggie, all I want to know is where do I stand with you, do you want to be with me or not?"

"Jasmine, I don't understand why you are trying to give me an ultimatum. I explained to you when we met that I didn't want to be in a committed relationship. And to answer your question - it is out of convenience. Now, if you're done questioning me, I have to go meet someone."

"Since you are being matter-of-fact and nonchalant with your responses, I guess I am done. We are excused to go meet whoever you're trying to meet."

As soon as the conversation between Jasmine and Reggie ended, Jasmine hung up her phone and ran directly to Sheila's room to tell her what she and Reggie spoke about. "Hey, Sheila are you busy?"

"No, I'm not, just checking some of my students' papers, come on in. What do you need?" "I need to talk." "Talk about what?"

"I was just on the phone with Reggie and while we were talking, I asked him where I stood with him. After I asked him, he told me that I already knew, from the first time we met, he didn't want to be involved in a serious relationship. Before I knew it, one thing led to another, and we ended up arguing."

"Girl you need to dump him. He's no good for you, and may I remind you that you can do better than him. You need to find someone like my James. Someone who will treat you like a queen and do anything for you."

"Sheila that sounds good, but I don't want anyone that will be a doormat that I can walk all over."

"Jasmine are you serious? Men do it to us women all the time."

"Again, that's not me. Sheila, I simply want someone who will respect and love me for me, that's all."

"Okay, now that you've said all of that, what are you going to do?"

"I'm going to wait and see what Reggie will do based on the ultimatum that I gave him about committing to me or we are done."

"We'll see. No disrespect but if that's all, you wanted to discuss, I have to get back to grading these papers."

"Oh, I'm done and Sheila thanks for always lending a listening ear." That night Jasmine sat in her room wondering to herself if Reggie would ever commit to being solely with her.

Jasmine hadn't spoken to Reggie for three days. Curiosity was killing her. Therefore, Jasmine thought it was time to call Reggie and ask him if he had time to think about the conversation they had regarding their relationship.

"Hi Reggie, it's been a few days since we last spoke, and I was calling to first see how you were doing. How are you?"

"Everything is going good with me and no I haven't had time to think about our last discussion. I've been bogged down with a lot of projects at work."

"Reggie, I'm tired of constantly being on this merry-go-round disaster of a relationship with you. I feel as if all you do is take from me and never add anything to me. I need someone in my life that will treat me like the queen I am. If you're not willing to give that to me, then we are done."

"Jasmine I don't have time for this today, I'll talk to you later once you've calmed down. Bye!"

Coming to the realization that it was senseless to threaten a person like Reggie with an ultimatum, Jasmine decided to stop hounding him and to allow things in their relationship to play themselves out. Jasmine also thought it was time to redirect her energy by focusing more on herself and her career goals. She still had no clue that the main reason Reggie refused to commit to her was because he had fallen for another woman. However, she would soon discover who the mysterious person was.

CHAPTER 17

One day when Jasmine returned home from work, she noticed that Reggie's car was parked outside her apartment building. While walking to her apartment, Jasmine thought it was strange that Reggie would be at her house since it had been several days when they last spoke to one another. As soon as Jasmine walked into the apartment, she noticed that Reggie was snuggled up with Sheila on the sofa.

"Hi Reggie, what are you doing here? I thought you were too busy with work to see me."

"Oh, hi Jasmine I thought since I was able to get off work early today, I would surprise you by stopping to see you. Do you have a problem with that?"

"No, the only problem I'm having right now is that you didn't tell me in advance that you were going to stop by to see me and the mere fact that you are sitting so close to Sheila on the couch in the dark."

While Jasmine and Reggie were talking, Sheila took it upon herself to join in on the conversation. "Babe I'm tired of sneaking around her back, tell her the real reason why you stopped by here."

Suddenly the conversation between Jasmine and Reggie shifted to Jasmine and Sheila. "What is all this babe stuff about?" "Did I stutter? I was perfectly clear in what I said." Sheila said sternly.

"Wow, now everything is making sense! You are the reason why Reggie wouldn't commit to me. Sheila, how could you do this to me, and right under my nose. I thought you were my best friend. I thought we were more than best friends. I thought we were sisters."

"Yea we were like sisters, but the heart wants what the heart wants. Jasmine how could you blame me, Reggie is so fine, smart and rich. And now he's all mine!"

"What do you mean, he's all yours?", Jasmine exerted.

"Jasmine, you might as well get over it, because Reggie is my man and I'm pregnant with his baby and there's nothing you can do about it," Sheila smugly answered.

Jasmine stood motionless and unable to speak. Sheila, the one person who had been her constant support, was having an affair with Reggie behind her back and was now pregnant with his child.

"You know what Jasmine I've never really cared for you. You too weak, naïve and a little on the stupid side when it comes to men. Ever since high school you've never known how to pick the right man, let alone keep him."

Hearing Sheila say such horrible things to her, Jasmine's speechless demeanor suddenly transformed into anger. "Sheila, since you say I don't know how to pick the right person to date, why have been you sleeping with Reggie, someone you claim you couldn't stand to be around. By the way isn't Reggie the same person you told me was no good for me? And since we are talking about men, what happened with James? Does he know you've been fooling around with Reggie?"

"At this point in time my relationship with James is not up for discussion."

"That's fine because you'll get what's coming to you. Sheila, since you have betrayed my trust and my name is the only name on the lease, I think it's time that you move out!"

"What are you talking about, I'm not moving anyway. The only way you're going to get me out of here is by an eviction. And Jasmine, I already know you don't have the guts to put me out."

"Okay, if that's how you want to play this game, then so be it."

While Jasmine and Sheila went back and forth arguing about Reggie, he stood silently on the sidelines watching them go at it.

Realizing that her relationship with Reggie and her friendship with Sheila were both officially over, Jasmine knew it was time to sever all ties with them.

Hence, the next day Jasmine did just as she said she would do and went to the county courthouse to have eviction papers served on Sheila. On that day Jasmine erased all of Reggie's contact information out of her cellphone, threw away everything he had ever given her and had the lock to her apartment door rekeyed.

Nevertheless, shortly after Sheila was evicted from Jasmine's apartment she moved in with Reggie. However, her stay with him was short lived. Sheila succumbed to the same stress that Reggie imposed on Jasmine, his cheating ways. Sheila died resulting from an uncontrolled hemorrhage during a miscarriage of their child.

Through a mutual friend, Jasmine discovers that Sheila died, and her death came as a shock. She begins to blame herself, believing that she was the cause of Sheila's premature death.

A SHADE OF DARKNESS

In the Darkness Trouble Stirs

CHAPTER 18

The tragic end to her relationship with Sheila, especially because of this worthless man, is just too much. Jasmine goes off on the deep end. She feels a sense of guilt because their friendship ended horribly. There was no closure, she never got the opportunity to forgive Sheila or vice versa.

Because of the guilty feelings that Jasmine has been harboring, she begins to go to clubs and bars so much that many of the bartenders and bouncers know her by name. One evening, while having a glass of wine at Blues Bar and Grille, she crossed paths with Damien. Damien was an okay looking kind of guy but was not who he portrayed himself to be.

"Hi beautiful. Is someone sitting here?" Jasmine hesitated to respond as she thought to herself, what does he want? "No one is sitting there."

"What's a beautiful lady like you doing sitting all alone in a bar like this?"

"You ask a lot of questions for someone who just wanted a seat," Jasmine says sarcastically.

"My apologies, I didn't mean any harm. I thought since you were sitting at the bar by yourself, I would come over and keep you company, but if you don't feel like being bothered, I'll leave you alone."

"Now, I need to apologize to you for being rude. I'm sorry if I offended you and what is your name again?"

"I'm Damien Scott and your name?" "Pleasure to meet you Damien Scott, I'm Jasmine Sawman."

"Hi Jasmine Sawman, if I'm not being to presumptuous what are you doing here?"

"Well, to answer your question, I left work early and didn't quite want to go home, so I decided to stop in to have a drink. And I've been here ever since."

"If you don't mind, may I buy you a drink, something to eat or both?" "Oh, you don't have to."

"Don't worry, I want to do it," Damien stated.

"Since you insist, I won't mind having a basket of spicy honey garlic wings. I heard their wings here are good."

"Okay, your wish is my command." Jasmine and Damien sat in Blues Bar and Grille for the remaining of the evening, getting to know one another.

"So Jasmine, what is it that you do for a living?" "Um, I work for a major marketing firm. You may have heard of it, the Centél Firm." "Unfortunately, I haven't." "And what is it that you do?" "Oh, I work in sales."

For a moment Jasmine thought to herself that it was strange that Damien worked in sales but had no knowledge of the Centél Firm, a major marketing firm within the corridor of Atlanta that works with professionals in the sales industry.

Nevertheless, as the evening continued Jasmine and Damien drunk several drinks and discussed various topics, until Jasmine realized that it was late, and she needed to go home because she had to be at work early the next morning.

"Damien, it was nice meeting you and thank you for the drinks and food. It's late and I think it's time I go home."

"Since you've been drinking, do you think it would be wise that you drive yourself home?"

"You know what, you are absolutely right, I'll call for a taxi to take me home."

"If it's okay with you, I wouldn't mind taking you home." "Oh, that is sweet of you. But I don't want to inconvenience you, I'll just call for a taxi."

"It's not a problem for me and besides it will give me more time to get to know you better. By the way where do you live?"

"I live off Ponce de Leon near Linwood Avenue, do you know the area?"

"I know exactly where that is. My buddy Mike doesn't live too far from you. If everything is okay with you, I'll pay the bill and we can go. Also, I'll let the manager know that you'll be back in the morning to retrieve your car."

"Thanks again for all your help, I'm glad I stopped here today."

As Jasmine and Damien proceeded to walk out of the restaurant, Damien jokingly said, "Yes because you would have never met me."

Jasmine chuckled at Damien's statement and silently said to herself, "yea right." However, before the evening ends Jasmine will discover Damien's true intention.

CHAPTER 19

As Damien approached Jasmine's apartment complex, Jasmine realized that she had left the gate key in her car at the restaurant. Because Jasmine didn't have her gate key, Damien told her that he would park his car and walk her to her door and Jasmine agreed.

When Jasmine and Damien arrived at her apartment, she thanked him for ensuring that she made it home safely. However, the moment Jasmine opened her door Damien, without warning, he pushed her inside the apartment and began to rape her.

During the entire assault Jasmine tried her best to fight Damien off, but he was too strong for her. As soon as the attack was over Damien got dress and before he exited Jasmine's apartment, he threatened her: *"If I find out that you told anyone what happened here tonight, you will regret it. Don't forget I know where you live and where you work."*

Frightened by what had just happened to her and too afraid to move because of the threat made by Damien, Jasmine spent the rest of the night balled up in a fetal position on her living room floor. The following morning when Jasmine woke up, she thought she had a night terror, but after she saw her face and clothes, she realized that she had been raped.

Once Jasmine came to grips with what happened to her, she immediately got in the shower and attempted to wash all the stench of Damien from her body. When Jasmine got out of the shower she sat on the side of her bed and weep uncontrollably; however, amid her tears, she realized that she was not going to be able to make it to work and needed to call out on sick leave.

After Jasmine called her supervisor at the Centél Firm, she informed her that she had an emergency in her family and needed a few days off from work. She then called the management at her apartment complex to have maintenance change out the locks on her doors. Jasmine also went out and purchased a hand gun and had security cameras installed in and around her apartment.

With all the measures that Jasmine had taken to safeguard herself from the possibility that Damien would come back to assault her again, it didn't ease her sense of security. She became so paranoid that she began to sleep with the lights on with the gun underneath her pillow.

Overtime the weight of having been raped starts to affect Jasmine. She wants so desperately to tell someone what happened to her, but she has no one she can trust. Jasmine couldn't call Sheila because she is dead. She couldn't call her parents because they will worry. And she couldn't call her sisters, Ashely and Allison, because they were no longer close to each other.

After several months of walking around with the tormenting secret that she was raped by a person she had met at a bar, Jasmine decided it was time that she reported the assault to the police and got some counseling before she went insane.

CROSSROADS

*Decisions are Difficult to Make
When Two Paths Cross*

CHAPTER 20

The moment Jasmine gained the confidence to report her rape, she was victimized all over again. The questioning by the investigating officer who took down Jasmine's statement of the assault made her feel, through insinuation, that it was somehow her fault that she was raped.

From this encounter Jasmine decided that she would not speak about her experience anymore. Jasmine's silence only pushed her into a deep state of depression. She began to drown her sorrows in bottles of wine. Jasmine's drinking became so excessive that she drunk wine every day, from sunrise to sunset.

After existing this way for some time, Jasmine was again sitting in her apartment, drinking a glass of wine, when she began to reflect over the past few years of her life and wondered how she ended up in this place. Several thoughts crossed her mind. Jasmine thought to herself that maybe Sheila was right when she told her that she didn't know how to pick the right kind of guy.

Jasmine also thought it was too late to pray to God and ask him to help her forget about Damien and the rape because it had been several years since she last attended church. Each time a negative thought crossed Jasmine's mind, she would drink another glass of wine. Before the night had ended, Jasmine had consumed so much wine that she passed out across her bed.

When Jasmine woke up the next morning, tortured by a severe hangover, the same thoughts replayed in her head from the previous night. She realized it was time that she reached out to someone for help. Jasmine researched on the internet and found a rape crisis hotline and called them.

And from that telephone call she was directed to Dr. Teresa Boatman, a licensed therapist whose expertise was working with women who have been assaulted. As soon as Jasmine called Dr. Boatman's office, she was scheduled for an appointment the next day.

Not knowing what to expect, Jasmine went to her scheduled appointment to meet with Dr. Boatman. Upon her arrival Jasmine was introduced to Dr. Boatman. "Good morning Miss Sawman, it is a pleasure to meet you. What is it that I can help you with today?", Dr. Boatman inquired. For a few seconds Jasmine sat in silence before she responded to Dr. Boatman's inquiry.

Suddenly Jasmine responded with tears streaming down her face and said," I've been raped, and I don't have anyone I can trust to talk to. Can you please help me, I don't like the way I've been feeling since the assault happened? I feel like I'm going crazy or something. Sometimes I feel like I want to kill myself because I can't escape the fact I've been raped and the person who did it won't be punished for it."

"Yes, Miss Sawman I can help you," Dr. Boatman replied.

"Thank you so much Dr. Boatman, you don't understand what this means to me," Jasmine replied.

The session went on for another forty-five minutes, however, before the session ended Dr. Boatman explained to Jasmine that her issues ran deep and one session with her would not get to the root cause of her feelings of depression and anxiety.

Dr. Boatman also prescribed her some anti-depressants to treat her depression and valium to help her sleep at night. She had her secretary to schedule Jasmine for a series of follow-up visits. As Jasmine proceeded to leave Dr. Boatman's office and internalize all the information she shared with her from their initial session, Jasmine thought that the rape was the problem she needed help with overcoming, not realizing that she had some other unresolved issues from her past.

Over the next several months Jasmine attended her therapy sessions with Dr. Boatman. At each session Jasmine poured out her feelings and disclosed how she felt inadequate as a person because she continuously picks the wrong type of man to date. There was also the guilt complex she had stemming from having sex at an early age and getting pregnant only to miscarry. And now how she felt about being raped.

She also revealed that outside of being friends with Sheila when she was alive and the demise of their friendship, she had no other real friends or support system in Atlanta to help her make it through the healing process.

After hearing what Jasmine had to say about her thoughts and feelings, Dr. Boatman prescribed an unorthodox remedy.

Dr. Boatman instructed Jasmine to take a trip home to visit her parents. By doing so, she would get some much-needed rest surrounded by familiar faces. She could get closure by visiting Sheila's grave to express her feelings. Dr. Boatman also suggested that she begin journaling her thoughts and to call her every week until she could return to the office for a regular visit.

They could then talk about any breakthrough or feelings she was experiencing while visiting her parents. Jasmine was not at all thrilled by the prescription given by Dr. Boatman to go home to visit her parents in Swainsboro, but she knew it would be good for her to return to her roots.

CHAPTER 21

As soon as Jasmine got home from her appointment with Dr. Boatman, she thought it was time that she called her parents to have a talk with them. "Hello mom this is your baby girl, how are you doing?"

"Hi baby, it's so good to hear from you, how have you been? And why haven't you returned any of our phone calls, your father and I have been so worried about you? Is everything okay with you?", Peggy asked.

"Okay, okay mom how many questions are you going to ask me? Everything is okay, where's dad?"

"Jasmine, I'm just so glad to hear from you. As for your father, he's in the room asleep. He's been a little under the weather lately."

"Mom, how long has dad been sick?" "I didn't say he was sick, I said he was just not feeling well for the past few days."

"Well to me that sounds like he's sick. Has he been to see a doctor to find out what's going with him?"

"Now who's asking all the questions. Yes, we have called the doctor and scheduled an appointment for next week."

"Okay that's good, what day?" "The appointment is next Thursday. Why, are you coming to go with us?"

"Well yes that's why I was calling to let you guys know that I was coming home to visit for a few weeks."

"Is everything okay with you?", Peggy asked.

"Not really, I do have some things going on in my life, but I don't want to discuss them right now over the telephone. I have to go now mom, please tell dad I said hello and I should be there in the next few days."

"Okay, sweetheart take care and make sure you call us before you hit the road to come home. And I'll make sure to tell your dad that you called and said hello. Love you and take care! Oh, wait a minute before I hang-up, I wanted to tell you that there's going to be a Singles Retreat at Freedom Willingness Baptist Church. You should consider attending while you are in town. You won't believe who's hosting it." "Who mom?", Jasmine asked. "Charles Buckman, you remember him."

"Yes, mom I remember him. If you are done, I need to go now because I have some things to do before I go to bed. I'll call you before I get on the road to head home."

"Alright then, I didn't mean to hold you up. I just thought I would let you know that you have something to do when you get here. Again, good night and I love you."

For the next few days Jasmine prepared to travel home to visit her parents. She completed her projects at work, submitted her sick leave paperwork, paid all her bills and packed her clothes for the number of weeks she would be gone. The day came for Jasmine to travel to Swainsboro, Georgia.

As promised, she called her parents, "Hi mom, I'm calling to let you and dad know that I was getting on the road now to come home."

"Okay sweetie, drive safely and make sure you pray before you leave. And Jasmine, thanks for coming home to go with us to your father's doctor appointment."

"No problem mom, it's my pleasure to. Besides, I was coming home for a visit anyhow. Well let me go and I'll see you in a few hours."

When Jasmine hung-up her phone, she said a silent prayer and got on the road. Jasmine listened to various inspirational podcasts and before she knew it, she was pulling up to her parent's home. As Jasmine was getting out of her car, she heard a familiar voice call from the distance. "Hey, is that little Jasmine Sawman?"

Unable to recognize who was calling her name, Jasmine stood perplexed until the person got closer to her. "Oh, my goodness that is you. Girl how have you been? Your mama didn't tell me you were moving back here."

"Hi Mrs. Pritchett, yes, it's me and no ma'am I'm not moving back home. I'm just here to visit for a while, I needed some time away from the hustle and bustle of city life."

"Well I hope you get some rest while you are here and if you get a chance stop by my house and visit with me. Also tell your mom to call me, I need to tell her something. Don't forget now!", Mrs. Pritchett insisted.

"No ma'am I won't, and I will make sure to come by your house to visit you while

I'm here." "Alright baby see you later," Mrs. Pritchett replied.

When the conversation between Jasmine and Mrs. Pritchett ended, Jasmine rang the doorbell to let her parents know she had arrived. "Jasmine you here already, that didn't take you that long at all. Do you need any help with unpacking your luggage?", Peggy asked.

"No, I don't need any help unpacking, just hold the door for me please." As Jasmine entered her parent's home, she asked her mother how her father was feeling since the time they spoke earlier during the day.

"Your father is awake, go to our room and let him know that you arrived safely."

"I will. Let me put my things in the room first. By the way which room will I be sleeping in?"

"Take the guess room because your old room has been transformed into my sewing room."

As Jasmine proceeded to walk up the stairs she turned around and said, "Oh mom I forgot to tell you Mrs. Pritchett saw me when I drove up and told me to tell you to call her when you get a chance."

"Thanks for telling me, I will make sure to do that."

Once Jasmine put her luggage up, she went to see her father. Prior to entering her parent's room, Jasmine knocked on the door and said, "Hello dad, it's Jasmine are you up?"

"Hello Jazzy, yes I'm up come on in," Carl replied.

"Dad how have you been, mom told me earlier this week that you have not been feeling well lately."

"That's true but I think it may be the flu or something."

"To be truthful dad, I don't think so you've lost too much weight for it to be the flu. I'm glad mom made you an appointment to see the doctor tomorrow because dad you don't look good to me."

"Sweet pea, don't worry. Everything will be okay you'll see."

"I hope you're right." Jasmine said in disbelief.

For the rest of the evening Jasmine and her parents sat and talked. At one point during their conversation Jasmine explained to her parents why she came home to visit them.

"Mom, dad I know the both of you are probably wondering why I came home to visit. But before I tell you, I want you to promise me that you won't overreact and start worrying."

"We promise." Her parents said in unison.

Jasmine took a deep breath and said, "A man broke into my apartment, robbed me and threatened to harm me if I called the police."

"Oh, no are you okay? Did you report it to the police? Did you change your locks?", Peggy asked.

"Mom, mom, calm down. Yes, on everything. See, this is the very reason why I didn't want to tell you about it because I knew you would flip out and panic," Jasmine answered.

"Good, I'm glad to hear that. Jazzy, we just want to make sure you reported it so the person can be caught," Carl said.

Carl and Peggy, have no clue that Jasmine was not being truthful with them about why she really came home to visit. Nevertheless, Jasmine and her parents talked a little longer and then went to bed.

CHAPTER 22

On the day of Carl's doctor's appointment, almost everyone in the house was calm and filled with positive vibes. Peggy tried her best to put up a good front so as not to alarm her husband that she worried about him. When the Sawman family arrived at Dr. Ackerman's office, they were led to the examination room. As Dr. Ackerman reviewed Carl's chart, he asked him why he came into the office. Carl described his symptoms he had been experiencing for the last few weeks.

Based on the information that Carl shared with him and the details from a physical examination, Dr. Ackerman had his nurse to draw his blood to test for different diseases. Before Carl left the doctor's office, he was informed that as soon as his test results returned, he would be notified.

For the next several days, the atmosphere in the Sawman's household was intensive. Everyone walked around on edge, wondering what the test results would reveal about Carl's health. Dr. Ackerman's office finally received the results of Carl's blood test and they were not favorable. Because of the nature of Carl's test and the severity of the results, Dr. Ackerman did not want to discuss the results over the telephone.

Therefore, he had his assistant contact Carl to inform him that the results from his blood work were back and he needed to come into the office to hear the findings.

Unsure of what the results would reveal, Carl insisted that he, Peggy and Jasmine say a prayer before they went into Dr. Ackerman's office to speak with him.

Although the Sawman family prayed that the results of Carl's test would be favorable, the results showed that he had stage two pancreatic cancer and would need to immediately undergo several rounds of chemotherapy and have surgery to remove any cancer that chemo didn't destroy.

After hearing the devastating diagnosis that the person they called husband and dad was sick with cancer, and could possibly die,

Peggy and Jasmine were in dismay. However, Carl remaining calm and poised, told Dr. Ackerman that whatever it took to get well he was ready. He would go forward with the proposed treatment plan. From the news of Carl's diagnoses, Peggy thought it was time for the entire family to come together to pray.

For Jasmine, however, the news of her father's cancer diagnoses, and the realization that she would soon be surrounded by her sisters, triggered her anxiety. Based on how she began to feel in such a short period of time, Jasmine knew she needed to call Dr. Boatman before she sunk back into a dark place of despair.

"Hello Dr. Boatman, this is Jasmine Sawman. You told me that while I was visiting my parents to call you if I started to experience any feelings of anxiety or depression. Well, because of the recent news my family received about my father's health, my feelings of normalcy have gone south. I don't think me coming home was a good idea. With everything that's going on down here, it's too hard for me to cope."

"Miss Sawman, I understand what you are feeling but may I suggest that since your father's health is on the decline that you give yourself more time being around family before you decide to return to Atlanta. While you've been down there, have you had time to visit your friend's grave?", Dr. Boatman inquired.

"No, I haven't but I will try to do so in the next few days, if I get a chance," Jasmine answered.

Before the conversation between Jasmine and Dr. Boatman ended, Jasmine was advised to continue taking her anti-depressants and, if she had any further problems, to call Dr. Boatman's office.

As suggested by Dr. Boatman, Jasmine decided to remain in Swainsboro and within three weeks, things for Jasmine and her family went from bleak to bright. Her father's surgery was a success and it would seem he was reacting well to his chemotherapy treatment. Throughout this process, Jasmine spent most of her time relaxing and helping her mother take care of her father.

Jasmine had an opportunity to visit Sheila's grave to express her feelings of forgiveness on how their friendship abruptly ended on a sour note. Additionally, Jasmine had a chance to reconnect with an old childhood friend. One day while running errands for her mother, Jasmine bumped into

Charles Buckman. "Hi, Jasmine good to see you. It's been a longtime since we last saw each other. How have you been?", Charles asked.

"Oh, everything is okay. And how's life been treating you?"

"Pretty good, pretty good. I can't complain. You know I had no clue you were in town. How long have you been here?"

"Well, I came home for a short vacation to spend time with my parents but decided to stay a little longer when we found out my father was sick," Jasmine replied.

"I'm so sorry to hear that. Is there anything I can do to help?"

"Not really, just keep my family in your prayers. I have to go now I still have some errands to run for my mother. It was good seeing you though, take care."

"It was good to see you as well. Jasmine if you have time this weekend, I would like to invite you to the Singles Retreat I'm hosting at my church," Charles suggested.

"And which church would that be?" "Freedom Willingness Baptist Church over on Richman Road, activities will begin Friday night at 7 o'clock."

"My mom told me about that retreat before I came home. How long have you been attending church there?"

"I've been there since I came on staff as an Associate Pastor about two years ago." "Oh, okay I will try to come. Thanks for the invite."

"Take care and I hope to see you this weekend. Tell your parents I said hello and that I'm praying for them."

"I sure will. And I'll try my best to make it to the retreat. See you later."

All week long, Jasmine went back and forth in her mind about whether she would attend the Singles Retreat being hosted by Charles. However, after having a heart-to-heart conversation with her father about life, finding love, and happiness, Jasmine decided that she would take a chance and attend at least the first night of the retreat.

After taking that leap of faith, Jasmine had such a good time the first night of the retreat, reconnecting with people from her youth when she participated in the sunshine youth group at New Life Holiness Church. She attended all three nights.

Jasmine's decision to attend the retreat proved to be good for her. So good in fact that her perspective about life began to shift and become more positive. Unfortunately, Jasmine's sick leave was coming to an end and she had to make a difficult decision; whether she would remain in Swainsboro to help her mother care for her father or return to her life in Atlanta.

THE CROSS OF REDEMPTION

Redemption comes through Forgiveness

CHAPTER 23

Although Jasmine desires to remain in Swainsboro to assist her mother with the care of her father, she knows she must return to Atlanta if she wants to maintain her position at the Centél Firm and resume her therapy sessions with Dr. Boatman. Because of this reality, Jasmine decided that before she returned to her life in Atlanta that she would spend her last week treating her parents to scrumptious meals at the finest local restaurants and mini excursions in Savannah, Georgia.

Jasmine's last week at home flew by so quickly that the weekend before she was due to leave, she thought she would surprise her parents by attending Sunday service at New Life Holiness Church with them.

During the service at New Life Holiness Church, Jasmine and her parents had the privilege to hear the Reverend Dr. Eli Peterson preach his last sermon prior to his retirement after 45 years of pastorship of the church.

Dr. Peterson's last sermon was based on Romans 4:25 and entitled, "Forgive Thyself and Live." As the Reverend Dr. Peterson began to preach, Jasmine sat still and listened intently to every word he spoke, especially when he covered the part of scripture that Jesus gave up his life for the sins of others and was raised to life to make people right with his Father.

The entire time Jasmine listened to Dr. Peterson preach, tears flowed down her face. She knew deep within that the sermon was somehow meant for her to hear. When Dr. Peterson finished delivering the message, he called for those in the congregation who had been holding unforgiveness toward themselves for past indiscretions to come to the altar for prayer.

Jasmine didn't move immediately, but realizing she needed to move, she got up after the second call and went down to the altar for prayer.

When every person who heard the call for prayer responded, Rev. Dr. Peterson began to pray:

"We come to you O'Lord on behalf of your people. Asking that you will forgive them of their sins, heal their hearts and minds, and give them the strength to let go of all bad choices they have made in their past due to immaturity or ignorance. We pray, Father God, that each of your people who are gathered here at the altar and those who remain at their seats, may they, according to your word in Isaiah 61:3, receive beauty for their ashes. May their lives, Lord God, never be the same and may they walk on a new path of being. We ask of these things in your precious and mighty name Jesus." -Amen-

After worship, Peggy saw Mother Thornton and they began to hold a conversation. Meanwhile Jasmine and her father sat in the vestibule of the church and waited on her to finish talking. Before Peggy ended her conversation with Mother Thornton, she motioned for Jasmine to come over where they were standing to say hello to Mother Thornton.

"Hello Jasmine. Good to see you, you know I was just asking your mother about you. It's been a long time since I last saw you. How has life been treating you?", Mother Thornton inquired.

"Hi Mother Thornton, apart from what we been through as a family regarding my father's health, I've been fine," Jasmine answered.

"Are you sure," Mother Thornton asked. "Yes ma'am, I'm sure."

"Okay if you say so. I can't argue about your feelings. Again, it was good to see you. Take care of yourself and the next time you come home to visit your parents, stop by and say hello to an old woman," Mother Thornton insisted.

As Mother Thornton turned to walk away from Peggy and Jasmine, she said, "Jasmine, the Lord says he has forgiven you and it's now time for you to forgive yourself."

Looking perplexed Jasmine hesitantly responded *"okay"* because she knew what Mother Thornton had just told her was confirming what the pastor had preached earlier in the day.

Later that day, after Jasmine and her parents ate dinner, she went outside and sat on the porch of her parent's home to reflect on what Rev. Dr. Eli Peterson had spoken about at church, and the last thing Mother Thornton said to her before she left church.

After sitting for nearly an hour, a thought crossed Jasmine's mind to write a letter to herself as an outer expression of how she felt about herself. The letter would also serve as a mechanism to express forgiveness to herself for all the mistakes she made thus far in life. Jasmine spent the rest of the night on the porch jotting down points she would cover in her letter of forgiveness to herself.

CHAPTER 24

It was the next morning before Jasmine had completed her letter of forgiveness. Writing the letter to herself, Jasmine experienced some feelings she had not encountered before, not even while attending therapy sessions with Dr. Boatman.

It would seem as though Jasmine had a breakthrough. She was finally on the road toward truly being healed of her past. She was now willing to forgive herself as Christ had already forgiven her of her transgressions.

By writing the letter of forgiveness, Jasmine realized that it was not the fault of her parents, who were God-fearing, that she made bad choices in her life. Most of the things she faced in her relationships with men were partially a result of low self-esteem, a lack of self-love and the inability to forgive others for what they had done to her.

Jasmine also came to the realization from writing the letter that most of the time when she dated, she gave up a valuable piece of herself, which eventually led to her heart being trampled and stomped on. In short, Jasmine learned that the relationships she had formed with the men of her past were relationships of convenience and she had to admit to herself that there was no more room or time for her to compromise the qualities she knew she deserved out of a man.

By the end of writing her forgiveness letter, Jasmine concluded the she could no longer date anyone who didn't possess the essence of God, and that the person she chose to date had to be willing to embrace her shortcomings and the things she wanted out of life.

Furthermore, Jasmine had to grasp the fact that she deserved the best that life had to offer her, that she was wonderfully and marvelously made in the image of God; and that she needed to take time out to get to know herself better.

A Letter of Forgiveness

Dear Jasmine,

   Please forgive me for all the times I displayed poor judgment in the men I allowed you to be involved with and failing to realize that your validation and affirmation does not come from man but from God Forgive me for allowing your spirit to intertwine with so many immature and boyish individuals who I thought were men and sharing important information with people about those relationships. I say to you on this day that I can no longer allow you to defile your body with sharing a precious and valuable part of your spiritual being with a man to whom you are not married to.

   Jasmine it is my desire for you to be with someone who not only wants you but wants all of you to include your shortcomings, past mistakes and that which God has for your future. It is my prayer for you that you will no longer be attracted to men who will use your love to manipulate you to achieve a sexual relationship. Jasmine, please allow God to lead and reveal to you the things that he has preordained for you to accomplish in your life and in the earth. Jasmine as you await the arrival of the man that God has designed specifically for you take time out and date yourself and get in-touch with your inner-self. Today you are forgiven, walk in freedom.

Loving You More,
Jasmine

Jasmine's letter of forgiveness brought her to a place of freedom and liberation. A place where she could begin to live a more fulfilled life as God had intended for her and to think positively about herself. When Jasmine had completed writing her forgiveness letter, she prayed a silent prayer:

"Hello Jesus, this is Jasmine. I know it has been a while since the last time I prayed to you and I apologize for that. Before I ask you for anything, I want to say thank you for standing in the gap for me with Father God. Lord Jesus, if it's not too much, I pray that now I have decided to forgive myself as you have already forgiven me, that you will grace me with the fortitude and insight to live a more joyous and productive life, centered not just on my career goals but on you and my family."

As Jasmine summed up her prayer, she asked God that he would bless the efforts behind her forgiveness letter and give her a life that was more reflective of how he desired for her to live instead of the way she had been living; and that she would have a bright future filled with endless possibilities of love and hope.

CHAPTER 25

Since Jasmine had spent the whole night writing her forgiveness letter, she thought she would take a nap before she got on the road to travel back to Atlanta. Before Jasmine laid down to sleep, she asked her mother to wake her up in a few hours, so she could get on the road before it got too late. After about five hours of sleeping Jasmine was up from her nap and ready to head back to Atlanta.

As Jasmine prepared to leave, her mother told her that once she arrived at her apartment in Atlanta to give her a call to let her know she got there safely. Later that same day when Jasmine had arrived at her apartment, she called her mother, as promised, and informed her that she made it back safely.

"Hi mom, I'm calling to let you know that I made it back safely."

"Okay, that's good to hear. I don't want to hold to you too long because I know you may be still tired. Get some rest and I'll talk to you later," Peggy replied.

"Alright mom, could you tell dad I made it safely and I'll talk to the both of you later."

"I sure will, and you get some rest, you hear. Take care and I love you." "Okay, bye."

When Jasmine ended her conversation with her mother, she went room by room checking to make sure every door and window in the apartment was secured. Realizing that everything in her apartment was okay, Jasmine laid out her clothes for work and prepared for bed.

The following day when Jasmine arrived at work, she received the shock of her life, she discovered that the project she and her teammates presented prior to her sick leave, won a multi-million-dollar marketing contract for the Centél Firm.

Because Jasmine's team acquired such a large contract, each member on the team was promoted to a higher position within the company. It would seem as though Jasmine's path in life was getting brighter.

A BECKON OF HOPE

There is always a light luminating at the end of a dark tunnel

CHAPTER 26

Once again, just when everything in Jasmine's life was improving and on a positive track tragedy visits her doorstep. No sooner than Jasmine had returned to Atlanta and settled into her new role as Marketing Director at the Centél Firm, and successfully ended her therapy sessions with Dr. Boatman, she received a phone call from her sisters Ashely and Allison telling her she needed to return to Swainsboro immediately. Jasmine knew something was wrong because her sisters had never called her for anything.

"Hi Jasmine, this is Ashely. We just got off the phone with mom and she wanted us to call you to tell you to come home," Ashely stated.

"Who is we? Who else is on the phone with you?", Jasmine inquired. "Oh, Allison is on the other end," Ashely replied. "Hi Jasmine," Allison responded.

"Oh, hi Allison. What's going on? What's so important that I need to go home immediately? You may not realize it, but I literally just came from there a few weeks ago. Why do I need to go back so soon? Is there something wrong with dad?", Jasmine asked.

"We don't know, all we know is that we all need to go home," Ashely answered.

"It's only been a short time since I last took off, I'll need to see how much time I have available for leave. I'll go the day after tomorrow," Jasmine suggested.

"Really Jasmine, I just told you mom wants all of us to come home immediately and all you have to say is you have to find out how much leave time you have!"

"Look, I'm not doing this with you Ashley. How can you call me now and tell me to get home and you can't call me any other time? If you are done, I must go now," Jasmine insisted.

"Okay Jasmine, just like you said we're not going there with you either. The only reason we called you was because mom wanted us to call you. Since it is going to take you some time before you can go home, I suggest you call mom and tell her yourself that you'll be there in a few days," Allison interjected.

"Thanks for calling and I'll call mom to tell her what I just told you," Jasmine replied.

Just like Jasmine told her sisters before she ended her call with them, she called their mother to inform her that it would be a few days before she was able to come home. When Peggy found out that Jasmine was not on her way home as she was instructed, she was disappointed. "Hi mom." "Hi Jazzy, are you on the way home?", Peggy inquired.

"No, that's why I'm calling you. It will be a few days before I'll be able to get there," Jasmine answered.

"And why is that, didn't Ashely and Allison tell you I needed all of you girls to come home immediately?", Peggy asked.

"Mom, in case you forgot, I was just there a few weeks ago and without any explanation you want me to come back. I do have new responsibilities at work that I can't neglect," Jasmine answered.

"Well the way your father and I raised you and your sisters that besides God nothing takes precedence over the affairs of family.

With that being said, I expect you to be here tomorrow," Peggy exerted.

Before Jasmine could respond to her mother's comments, Peggy had hung up the phone. Jasmine could not have foreseen that the reason why her mother summoned her daughters to come home was because there has been a sudden change in her father's health.

After two days, Jasmine finally headed home to find out why her mother wanted everyone to come there. However, before Jasmine was able to get home her father had unexpectantly passed away.

When Jasmine learned of her father's death, she couldn't fathom not having him in her life and once again was thrust back into a mode of depression, a familiar place of sadness and grief. On top of feeling sad, Jasmine felt guilty because instead of going home when she was asked to, she wasted time complaining to her mother and sisters on why she couldn't come.

CHAPTER 27

When Jasmine finally arrived at her parent's home, she was met with discontentment and it was days before anyone, especially her mother, would speak to her.

"Jasmine can you come here, I need to talk to you," Peggy stated. "Yes, ma'am coming," Jasmine replied.

"Jasmine come and have a seat. I know I haven't said anything to you since you got here, but I can no longer hold my peace. Jasmine I can't tell you how disappointed I am with you. You knew your father's health was poor. It didn't cross your mind that something could be wrong with him? All I want to know is why you didn't come home when I sent word for you to come?", Peggy asked.

With tears flowing down her face Jasmine responded, "Mom, I'm so sorry that I didn't come home when you asked me to come. You don't know how much I regret not getting here when you told me to. I didn't think it was that serious because I had just not too long-ago seen dad, and his health seemed to be getting better after his surgery."

"Jasmine, what I can't understand is that despite how your father and I raised you to keep Christ first in your life, to be respectable, loving and kind to others, and that family is important, you have become so selfish. Where did we go wrong with you? I gave you one simple request and that was to come home, but you couldn't because of your job," Peggy stated tearfully.

"Mom, how can you say that I'm selfish? When I took off time from work to come here and spent nearly a month to help with dad," Jasmine replied.

"No, let me correct you. You came home for a month, but you didn't come to help with your father, you came for yourself," Peggy answered.

"You may be right but when I came, it was with the hope that for once in my life the both of you would be there for me and help support me through some things I was dealing with at the time."

"What do you mean be there for you? We've always been there for you, even when we disagreed with your choices. You must have forgotten about the time you got pregnant by that no-good boy. What's his name? Demetrius, Donny, Dontrelle or something. Your father and I accepted the fact that our young and naïve daughter was going to be an unwed mother, which I remind you, went against our principles and how we raised you girls. We were willing at the time to do anything and everything to make sure you and your baby were well taken care of. Unfortunately, you miscarried and lost the baby. Who was there when that happened? We were! So, don't tell me about someone being there for you. Throughout this entire ordeal, we focused all our energy on you and not on your sisters!", Peggy exerted.

"I hear what you are saying but you don't understand mom, that I've been through some things as well, things that caused me to seek professional help to deal with my issues."

"What was going in your life that was so bad that you couldn't come to me or your father for help?"

For a moment, there was complete silence and then Jasmine blurted out, "You want to know why I came home? I came home because I was raped several months ago and since I had no one to talk to that would not judge me, I tried to commit suicide. Now you know, you happy?", Jasmine replied.

There was a point in the conversation between Jasmine and Peggy, the Rev. Dr. Peterson showed up at the Sawman home. "Um excuse me Sister Peggy, your door was open, and since no one answered when I knocked on the door, I decided to let myself in. I hope I'm not intruding, I can come back later if you would like me to."

"No need to apologize pastor, I'm done talking to Jasmine for now. What is it that I can help you with?"

"Oh, I just stopped by to see how you and the family were coping with the death of dear Brother Carl and to discuss his funeral service," Pastor Peterson stated.

"Thank you, Rev. Peterson for stopping by, I've been so busy with funeral arrangements and talking to family members on the phone that I forgot to call you. And to answer your question, we are trying our best to cope."

For the next hour Peggy and the Rev. Dr. Peterson sat and discussed the church service for her husband's funeral. When Peggy and the pastor finished talking, he asked if everything was okay with her and Jasmine.

"Sister Peggy, I noticed earlier as I approached your door that there was a lot of yelling between you and Jasmine. Is everything okay? Is there anything you care to discuss with me?", Pastor Peterson asked.

Before Peggy could answer Pastor Peterson's question, Jasmine rudely interrupted the conversation.

"To be honest Pastor Peterson, everything is not okay with us and things are definitely not okay with me. I finally thought I had come to a place of truth, a place of healing, a place of peace and then my father unexpectedly dies. And since his death I've been ridiculed because I didn't make it back here before he passed away. I feel like my mother and sisters blame me for his death. Nobody around here has a clue of what I've been through over the last few years of my life! I've apologized to my mother and I'm not going to do it again. I'm sad and mad that my father is no longer with us; he was the only person in the world who understood me."

"Jasmine, what in the world are you talking about? There is no way we blame you for the death of your father. Everyone knows your father had pancreatic cancer and recently suffered some complications because of his surgery. If anyone around here should be sad or angry, it should be me, I just lost my best friend of thirty-eight years. The only man I've ever loved in my entire life!", Peggy replied.

While Peggy was pouring her heart out, Jasmine received a revelation that she missed the mark for the promise she made to God, a promise to keep him and her family first. Realizing that she was wrong in the way she had been behaving since she arrived home, Jasmine asked her mother for her forgiveness and apologized for not coming home when she was asked to. As the Rev. Dr. Peterson excused himself, Jasmine and Peggy hugged and cried with one another.

CHAPTER 28

It was the day of Carl Sawman's funeral and everyone in the Sawman household was on edge because they knew the patriarch of their family would no longer be with them to celebrate birthdays, holidays, weddings or the birth of grandchildren.

Once the limousines from Stannis Funeral Home arrived, the family traveled to the homegoing celebration services of their beloved husband and father. When the family arrived at the church, they noticed how loved Carl was because nearly everyone in Swainsboro attended the funeral to pay homage to him. After the funeral and the burial of Carl, the family and their guests returned to New Life Holiness Baptist Church for the repast.

While Jasmine was sitting at a table waiting for funeral ushers to bring her a plate of food, Charles Buckman stopped by to give his condolences to her. "Hi Jasmine, I hope I'm not bothering you. I wanted to let you know how sorry I am that you loss your father. He was such an honorable and knowledgeable man; he will be greatly missed around here. Jasmine, if you should ever need someone to talk to, I'm here for you."

"Thank you Charles, that's kind of you but I'm okay."

"Jasmine I know this may not be the appropriate time or place to ask you this, but would you like to go out to dinner with me before you go back to Atlanta?" "And how do you know I live in Atlanta?", Jasmine replied.

"You forgot our mothers frequently talk to one another. So, would you like to go out to dinner with me?", Charles asked.

At the very moment that Charles asked Jasmine out to dinner, Mrs. Pritchett was passing by and overheard their conversation. Noticing that Jasmine was reluctant to say yes to his invitation to go on a date with him, Mrs. Pritchett jokingly whispered in Jasmine's ear, "baby if you don't go to dinner with him, I surely will. All jokes aside Jasmine, I truly believe that God fashioned that young man just for you. You may not see it now, but I believe over time you will. Honey, go ahead and say yes to his invitation to dinner."

As Mrs. Pritchett walked away, she said out loud, "Mark my word, you won't regret it!"

"Oh, Mrs. Pritchett, you are so funny," Jasmine chuckled.

"Well, Jasmine would you like to go to dinner with me?", Charles asked.

Taking into consideration what Mrs. Pritchett told her and the fact Charles asked her twice to go out to dinner with him, Jasmine hesitantly answered yes.

"Okay great. Jasmine, I don't want to take up anymore of your time from your family. If it's alright with you, I'll call you at your mother's house to set up the date and time that's best for you to go to dinner," Charles stated.

"Yes, that would be fine. Take care and I'll talk to you later," Jasmine replied.

Nevertheless, for the remainder of the day Jasmine sat and listened to family and longtime friends of her father share their memories of him.   For a brief moment while Jasmine listened to what everyone said about her father and how he impacted their lives, she wondered for the first time in her life what he would think about Charles if he were alive.

A SEASON OF RECOVERY

*There's a season and
reason for everything*

CHAPTER 29

Several days had passed before Charles contacted Jasmine to arrange their dinner date. At the time that Charles and Jasmine spoke they unanimously agreed that they would go to dinner the following day at 7:30 p.m.

The next day when Charles arrived to pick Jasmine up, he asked her if she didn't mind eating Chinese food at the Dragon Room and Jasmine said okay. While Charles waited on Jasmine to finish getting ready, he took some time to sit and talk to her mother to see how she had been coping since the death of her husband.

"Hello Mrs. Sawman, since I didn't get a chance to speak to you at your husband's funeral, I wanted to make sure I said something to you today. So, how have you been?"

"Sweetie, I still have days when I feel like I'm not going to make it, but God. You know this new normal is going to take me some time getting used to. But other than that, I am doing good, thanks for asking. Besides checking up on me, is there something I can help you with?"

"No ma'am, why do you ask," Charles answered.

"Well Charles, I know you didn't come all the way over here just to check up on an old lady like me," Peggy stated.

"Actually, I'm here to pick up Jasmine, we have a dinner date."

Just as Charles was explaining to Peggy the real reason why he stopped by her house, Jasmine walked into the room. "Okay Charles I'm ready if you are."

"Wow, don't you look pretty!", Peggy exclaimed.

"Thanks mom, I won't be out too late."
"Okay, you two have fun," Peggy responded.

Jasmine and Charles both simultaneously said, "We will." As the two proceeded to leave for dinner, Jasmine turned to Charles and said, "I didn't want to say this in front of my mom, but this is not a dinner date. Just so we are clear with one another, we are two old friends going out for dinner. That's all, get it," Jasmine responded.

"I understand, we are not going out on a date. We are just two friends going to eat some food and enjoy each other's company," Charles sarcastically replied. "Whatever Charles, let's go."

There was absolute silence in the car on the ride to the Dragon Room, until Charles asked Jasmine why she was so harsh toward him after he informed her mother that they were going on a dinner date.

"Jasmine, if you don't mind, can you explain to me why you were bothered when I told your mother we had a dinner date."

"Charles, I was simply stating that it was not a date. I apologize if you feel that my response to was too stern."

"By no means was I offended by your response to me. I just wanted to know, who or what hurt you so much in life that your demeanor has become so callous."

"You know what. Never mind, no comment. I promised that I would have dinner with you and that's just what we are going to do, so let's start over."

By the time Jasmine called a truce with Charles they had arrived at the Dragon Room. Jasmine and Charles spent the rest of their "not date" catching up with each other and talking about some of their future career plans.

"Jasmine, I know that you live in Atlanta but what do you do for a living?"

"What, my mother didn't tell your mother where I work? I'm shocked! Just kidding, I'm the Marketing Director at the Centél Firm."

"And what's the Centél Firm?" "We are a Fortune 100 marketing company with clients from the music to the fashion industry."

"Are you happy working there?", Charles asked.

"Absolutely, this is my dream job. I never thought in a million years that I would become the youngest executive at a company such as Centél. So, let me ask you some questions, where do you work and what do you do?", Jasmine inquired.

"Well for the last few years, after receiving my MBA, I've been working part-time as an Adjunct Professor at the local community college and I own a cleaning company and two laundromats," Charles answered.

"That's great! I'm impressed, I didn't know you had that going on. I truly thought that you were just working at your church."

"Yes, I do love the Lord and work in ministry, but I do have a career as well. Now that we've gotten all the preliminaries out of the way and we know what each other does, let's enjoy our food and each other's company."

With the night winding down, Charles asked Jasmine if he could call her once she got back to Atlanta and she agreed. By casually saying yes to Charles, Jasmine unknowingly sparked some old childhood feelings he once had for her.

CHAPTER 30

After a week of being home and helping her mother clear out some of her father's belongings, Jasmine returned to Atlanta. Once Jasmine got back to her apartment it suddenly hit her that she would no longer get a chance to hear her father's voice over the phone or gain his witty advice when she needed it.

Nevertheless, as Jasmine began to reacclimate herself into her everyday life in Atlanta, she thought it was time to get back to the business of living. She knew if her father were alive, he would tell her to go and live her best life. Therefore, as a form of living her best life, Jasmine enrolled into Judo, joined a gym and started rock climbing as a hobby.

As Jasmine continued to participate in her extracurricular activities on her quest to live an abundant life, she met an array of goal-oriented people who had similar ambitions. They, however, lacked one component that she so desired to have again and that was to have an intimate relationship with God.

One day while sitting on a bench in the courtyard of her apartment complex, Jasmine had a nudge. She thought to herself that if her father knew prior to his death that she had stopped going to church, he would be highly disappointed with her. Therefore, to honor her father's memory and what he taught her, Jasmine began to attend church.

Each time Jasmine attended church she would feel a sense of conviction because there were some things still festering within her that she had not surrendered to God. Over time, however, God revealed to Jasmine that she had a problem with trusting people and until she learned to do so she would always have an issue knowing who he designed for her.

Because of this revelation, Jasmine decided it was time that she come clean once and for all with God:

"Father God, I humbly come before your throne of grace by way of your Son Jesus Christ, my Lord and savior and to never forget the Holy Spirit. Lord God, I truly apologize and ask forgiveness for allowing the hurt of my past and how people mistreated me to cloud my judgement of how I now treat people in my life. Jesus, I need your help to get rid of these feelings of mistrust so that I can be open and ready to receive the person you have designed specifically for me and the people you will have me to meet or befriend. Father God, I also pray that if there are any other things in my life that still dwell within me that are displeasing to you, reveal them to me so that I can address them. In your precious and magnificent name Jesus the Christ."

Amen-

Just as Jasmine had finished praying, her cellphone rung, and it was Charles on the other end. "Hi Jasmine, this is Charles are you busy?" "Oh hey, I thought you forgot about me." "Why would you say that?", Charles asked.

"Well, maybe because it has been so many months since we last spoke."

As soon as Jasmine replied to Charles, the Holy Spirit pricked her spirit and she then realized that her response to Charles was not acceptable. Therefore, without hesitation Jasmine changed her tone and the way she was responding to Charles.

"I apologize for taking so long to call you, but I've been very busy lately with my businesses and the Singles ministry at church," Charles answered.

"That's perfectly fine, I know how hectic work can get and as a business owner I know things are even more difficult for you," Jasmine replied.

Jasmine and Charles spent so much time on the phone catching up with each other that before they knew it was nine o'clock at night. Before the conversation between them ended, he asked her if it would be okay if they prayed. "Jasmine are you there?", Charles asked.

"Huh? Oh yes, I'm here. What did you say?", Jasmine answered.

"I asked you if it would be okay if we prayed before we ended this call," Charles replied. There was a long pause before Jasmine answered Charles.

"I'm sorry Charles my mind wondered there for a minute. Yes, we can pray."

As soon as Charles began to pray, the first thing that came out of his mouth was,

"Father God, we come to you by way of your only begotten Son, Jesus Christ. Lord Jesus, it is my sincere prayer that you will heal your daughter's heart for being mishandled by the wrong people. And Lord may you equip her with spiritual discernment to recognize the people who truly want to see her happy and have the best that life has to offer her. In Jesus name we pray" -Amen

Just then Jasmine wondered to herself if Mrs. Pritchett was right when she told her that Charles was the man for her.

CHAPTER 31

Jasmine and Charles have been talking to each other on the phone for two months. It would seem as though every time they spoke their conversations got longer and longer. The conversations between them were so long that they would fall asleep on the phone with each other. One evening while they were talking, Jasmine asked Charles what qualities would his ideal wife possess and in response Charles jokingly answered, "Why do you want to be her?"

"Ha-ha, you wish! No seriously Charles, what qualities would you like your future wife to have?", Jasmine asked.

"I'll answer your question, if you answer mine." Charles responded. "And what question would that be?"

"What qualities do you wish your future husband to have?"

"I'll tell you what I want out of my husband, if you go first?"

"Since you insist that I go first, here it goes. My future wife must believe that Jesus is the son of God and have a personal relationship with him. Um, she must get along with my mother and sisters. She must respect the fact that I am involved in ministry and a business owner. My ideal wife needs to be able to cook. She doesn't have to be a culinary chef, but her cooking should be somewhat half-way decent. Also, my wife should have her own goals in life that she wants to pursue. Although these are the qualities I desire to have in a wife, I want the woman that God has uniquely designed for me."

"Wow that's a lot you want out of your wife," Jasmine replied.

"I've learned that when you ask God for something you have to be specific in your asking. Now it's your turn, what do you want out of your future husband?"

"You know I haven't really thought about it. I don't know what I want my future spouse to possess, but one thing I can say is he can't be anything like the men I've dated in the past," Jasmine replied.

"Have you ever thought about being with someone like me?", Charles asked.

"Absolutely not, you're too good of a friend to date."

"Why do women always consider guys like me to be a friend instead of someone they would date or marry. Whether you know it or not, the best relationships, like marriages, develop from friendships."

"Anyway, let me think. Hmm, I think I want a man who loves the Lord, a person who is career-oriented, who will treasure me for me. A man who will be committed and faithful to our relationship and family. I want someone who will marry my mind and not my body. Someone who will have my back when I hit my lowest point in life as well as when I'm at a place that's high with success. Lastly, I want a man who will love me despite my past."

"Sounds like you just described me," Charles jokingly replied.

"Really Charles, don't flatter yourself. I'm sorry I ever brought up this conversation." Feeling embarrassed, Jasmine attempted to change the conversation.

"No, no, no, I'm not going to let you off the hook that quick. There's a reason why you brought up this topic. Now tell me the truth Jasmine, why we are talking about what we want our future spouses to be like and marriage?"

"Charles, the only reason why I asked you what you wanted your ideal wife to be like is because now-a-days people in our age group are shying away from getting married. They are choosing to the play field or should I say hook-up instead of committing to a serious relationship like marriage. And since you are in ministry, I wanted to gain your perspective. That's why we are talking about marriage. But now I feel like this conversation is becoming a bit awkward."

"Jasmine, what's so awkward about us discussing marriage?"

"I don't know, but it's weird for two friends of the opposite sex to be talking about marriage. Can we just change the subject?"

Sensing that Jasmine was feeling uncomfortable, Charles changed topics. Jasmine and Charles spent the next two hours talking about various topics ranging from personal goals, politics to world events.

Jasmine had no clue that the many long nights talking to Charles was a set-up. Jasmine will soon discover that Charles had always wanted to date her but was too scared to approach her and tell her how he truly felt about her for fear of rejection.

LOVE DEFINED

*True Love Comes When You
Least Expect It*

CHAPTER 32

After several months of talking on the phone with one another, Jasmine and Charles' friendship was slowly shifting from something she was not expecting to something she greatly desired, true love. One evening during one of their usual calls, Charles summoned up the confidence and asked Jasmine if she wouldn't mind him coming to Atlanta to visit her for a week. Before she knew it, Jasmine said yes. When Jasmine came to her senses, and realized what she had said, she tried to explain to Charles that she made a mistake in her response to him.

However, it was too late because Charles excitedly exclaimed, "Cool, I was thinking about taking my vacation in the next few weeks. Would that be okay with you?"

Jasmine's response was not so enthusiastic, "Okay, I guess that would be fine."

"Why do you say it like that? You don't want me to come to visit you?" "No, Charles, that's not it."

"Well then, what is it? Can I come or not?", Charles asked.

"Yes, it would be okay if you came. I'm sorry if I sounded lackadaisical in my response. When did you say you were coming again?"

"That's okay, no harm, no foul. I accept your apology and I was thinking about coming in about two weeks. And Jasmine to ease your mind, I plan on staying in a hotel while I'm there."

As soon as Jasmine heard what Charles said, she let out a big sigh and told him to let her know when he was on his way to Atlanta. For the next few weeks Jasmine wondered to herself why would Charles want to come and visit her. Within two weeks' time Charles contacted Jasmine and informed her that he was on his way to Atlanta.

During their visit, Charles believed everything was going well. They enjoyed each other's company by visiting museums, going out to dinner, the movies and a local theme park. Although Jasmine seemed like she was having fun with Charles, he sensed something different.

After about four days of being around Jasmine, Charles began to feel some uneasiness coming from her. So, one day when they were preparing to go out on another city-wide adventure, he asked her why she had been stand-offish since his arrival.

"Jasmine, I've noticed that since I got here, you have not been that talkative. I'm getting the impression that you really don't want me to be here. Could my assessment be correct?"

"What are you talking about? Yes, I want you here. If I didn't, I would have told you when you first asked me if you could come and visit me. Also, if I didn't want you here, would I have taken time off from work to hang out with you?"

"Well no, but it does feel awkward to be visiting someone who won't talk to you and seems to be annoyed by your presence."

Without warning Jasmine yelled, "I already told you once that it was okay for you to be here. So, will you please stop saying that I don't want you here!"

"Look Jasmine I didn't come all the way up here on my vacation to get into an argument with you. I think it would be best if I cut my visit short and leave tomorrow," Charles replied.

"That's fine because I'm done trying to convince you that I want you to be here. Charles do what you want to do, I don't care anymore."

Shocked by the way Jasmine responded to him, Charles sat in silence and wondered to himself why Jasmine was treating him with so much contempt. Feeling uncomfortable, Charles decided that it was time to leave Jasmine's apartment. Being that Jasmine had picked him up earlier that day, Charles called for a taxi to take him back to his hotel. Shortly after Charles called for a taxi, it arrived and as he prepared to leave Jasmine's apartment, he told her," I'm sorry if my visit caused you any inconvenience. I hope this unpleasantry doesn't tarnish our friendship."

Despite Charles offering his apologies to Jasmine, she said nothing. Because of Jasmine's response or the lack thereof, Charles made it up in his mind that he would pray for Jasmine, maintain his distance but remain open to talk to her when she was ready to talk to him.

Once Charles left Jasmine's apartment, she realized that she was wrong for the way she responded to him. When she decided to run after Charles to catch him, it was too late because the taxi that came to pick him up had driven away.

The very next day Jasmine went to Charles' hotel to apologize to him and to explain why she responded the way she did toward him, but she missed him because he had already left. Realizing that it would take Charles some time to make it back home, Jasmine decided to wait a few hours before she tried to call him. After waiting nearly three hours to call Charles, Jasmine was finally able to contact him, but she didn't get the response she had hope for.

"Hi Charles, I came to your hotel room this morning to apologize for my behavior toward you but when I got there you had already gone." While Jasmine was talking, Charles remained silent.

"Hello, Charles are you there?", Jasmine asked.

"Yes, I'm here, go ahead and talk I'm listening," Charles replied.

"Well first, I want to apologize for telling you that it was okay for you to come all the way up here to visit me only to be unhospitable toward you. After spending all night thinking about it, I know I treated you the way I did because I was comparing you with the guys from my past who only treated me the way they did because they wanted something from me," Jasmine stated.

After a few minutes of hearing Jasmine offer her apology and reasoning for acting the way she did, Charles said to her, "I'm going to accept your apology, but the next time if there is a next time, could you please tell me what's bothering you instead going postal on a brother."

"Yes, I will do just that." "Okay, to respond to your other comment, could you please do me a favor and not box me in with those guys because I'm not like that. I only came to Atlanta to visit a friend and that was all. I didn't come with any other ulterior motives. Also, if I had a hidden agenda when I came to visit, I would have asked to stay at your apartment with you. Now since you opened the door to this discussion can I ask you a question Jasmine and you give me an honest answer." "Yes, what is your question?" "Based on your previous statement, do you see me as someone you would consider dating?"

"Charles, I'm not going to say no and I'm not going to say yes."

"So, what you are saying is maybe?" "I'm going to say maybe and leave it at that."

Nonetheless, as the conversation continued, Jasmine felt compelled to disclose to Charles one thing from her past that she had not shared with anyone except for her mother and therapist that she had been raped. She hoped that by telling him what she endured he would somehow understand why she was reluctant to give him a chance.

"Charles do you remember earlier in our conversation I shared with you the reason why I treated you the way I did while you were visiting me?"

"Yes, I remember. And do you remember what I told you?"

"Yes, you told me not to compare you with the men of my past because you are nothing like them."

"Jasmine what is it that you are trying to tell me?" Jasmine remained silent a moment and then said, "Charles the reason why I don't trust men, no matter how nice they appear to be to me, is because a guy I thought was nice raped me. Ever since that happened to me, I find it difficult to trust men."

"Jasmine I am sorry that happened to you, but like I told you I'm not like any man you've encountered. Because of that I would never hurt or do anything crazy that would cause you to mistrust me. Now that you have shared that part of your life with me, will you one day give me a chance?"

Based on the sincerity that Jasmine sensed coming from Charles throughout their conversation, she finally realized that Charles was a special of kind of man and thought it was time she gave him a chance to romance her.

CHAPTER 33

As time progressed Jasmine and Charles went from occasionally talking on the phone to video chatting every night. Because of all the interaction that occurred between the two of them, Jasmine began to see Charles in a different light. She began to develop feelings for him. She saw Charles as a man who genuinely cared about her, her feelings and what she wanted out of life. It would seem as though love was in the air and Jasmine and Charles' relationship had shifted from the friendship zone to becoming a full fledge couple.

From the very moment Jasmine and Charles became a couple, they made it a point to see each other as often as they could. Every two months either Charles or Jasmine was on the road traveling to see the other one.

The back and forth travel between Atlanta and Swainsboro went on for several months until it began to interfere with Jasmine's work travel.

One weekend while Jasmine was on a baecation in Tybee Island, Georgia, with Charles, she received an urgent last-minute message from Mrs. Harrison, her supervisor. She informed Jasmine that the Centél Firm was expanding their Marketing Division and they needed her to take the red-eye flight to London to assist with the expansion.

However, by the time Jasmine received the message and called Mrs. Harrison back to gain further details about her travel, it was too late, they had sent someone else in her place. After Jasmine learned that she had missed out on the greatest opportunity in her career her attitude toward Charles changed and he noticed it.

"Hey Jasmine, is everything okay with you?" "Yes, why do you ask?"

"I'm asking because ever since you got off the phone with your supervisor you've been quiet and moping around. Tell me what's

225

wrong with you?" "I just found out that I missed out on the ultimate career opportunity because I didn't receive an important message in a timely manner." "And what was the opportunity?"

"I was selected to travel to London to assist with the company's expansion plan for my division. Do you know what my involvement in this process could have done for my advancement within the company?"

"No, I don't but I have faith that you will get another chance."

"Look Charles I don't want to talk about this anymore, it's only making me get upset. Let's go and get something to eat?"

As not to further upset Jasmine, Charles switched subjects. "What is it that you want to eat?"

"I was looking at the reviews for things to do and places to go eat, and I saw that there were great reviews for the Coastal Seafood Restaurant. So, I think I would like to try some seafood."

"If you want seafood then seafood it is. Jasmine I hope you know how much I love you and want to help you realize all of your dreams."

"Yes Charles, I do realize that you love me, and I've known that since we reconnected as friends. But if I can be honest with you, I don't want our relationship to hinder my job. Therefore, I think we need to slow down on our bi-monthly commutes to see each other."

"If that's what you think is best for you then I guess we can."

Just before Jasmine and Charles left their rooms to go and eat, he told her that he's never seen anyone as complex and compound as her. After Charles made that statement, they both laughed. Jasmine and Charles enjoyed one another's company while they discussed ways they could continue to see each other without their visits interfering with Jasmine's travel work schedule.

CHAPTER 34

Except for some minor pitfalls, Jasmine and Charles's relationship had smoothly developed and it would seem as though marriage was on the horizon. One day while Charles was at the mall shopping for items for his upcoming trip with Jasmine to the Turks and Caicos Islands, he passed the window of a jewelry store and a ring that caught his eye.

When Charles went into the store to ask about the ring, he found that it was an engagement ring and it was on sale. Because Charles deeply loved Jasmine and felt that she was the one for him, he decided to purchase the ring so he could propose to her while on their trip. Jasmine had no clue that their vacation was going to be more than a vacation, it would be a surprise proposal trip.

A day before it was time for Charles to meet Jasmine in Atlanta, so they could fly out for their trip, Charles made it a point to go and see her mother in order to gain her permission to marry her daughter.

"Hello Mrs. Sawman, I hope I didn't catch you at a bad time?"

"Hi Charles, what a surprise. Come on in! Is everything okay?"

"Yes ma'am, everything is fine. Mrs. Sawman as you know Jasmine and I are leaving tomorrow for a short vacation. And since your husband is no longer with us, I thought it best if I came and asked you for your permission to marry Jasmine."

When Peggy heard the words marry your daughter, she immediately yelled with excitement, "Yes, yes, you have my permission to marry Jasmine! Charles I always thought that you and Jasmine would be perfect together. What took you so long to ask?"

"Thank you, thank you so much Mrs. Sawman you don't know what this means to me. I want you to know that I truly love Jasmine and I promise to never do anything that would harm her. I will treat her like the queen you and Mr. Sawman raised her to be and I'll make sure that she is well taken care of."

"You know Charles, I believe you but as for that second part of your statement good luck, you know how stubborn Jasmine is. I know you know by now how much she takes great pride in her work at the Centél Firm."

"Yes ma'am, I've discovered that since we first started dating."

"Charles, may I see the ring?" "Here it is, do you think Jasmine will like it?"

"Oh my, now that's a ring. Of course, she will, what woman wouldn't? By the way, how many carats is it?"

"It's a 3 carat Halo ring encased in rose gold."

"That's really a beautiful ring Charles. I don't want to take any more of your time, so call me when the both of you make it to your destination. And Charles, I'm more than certain that if my husband were alive, he would have been proud to have you as a son-in-law."

"Thank you again Mrs. Sawman and I can't wait to become a part of your family. Take care and I will make sure to call you once we arrive in Turks and Caicos Islands."

As Charles proceeded to leave his future mother-in-law's house, she asked him one last question. "Who else besides me knows that you are going to ask Jasmine to marry you?" He told Peggy that she was the only person who had knowledge of his intention to make Jasmine his wife. Once Charles answered Peggy's question, he left her house, so he could pack for his trip.

WHOLENESS

Two Halves Become One

CHAPTER 35

The following morning Charles got up early, so that he could get on the road to travel to Atlanta to meet Jasmine at the airport. When he arrived at the airport, Charles greeted Jasmine and tried his best to contain his composure. He didn't want to give away that he had a surprise for her once they arrived at their destination. Although Charles tried to act normal it was not working because Jasmine began to question him.

"Charles why are you acting so suspicious, what are you up to?"

"Nothing's up. I'm just excited to go on this island adventure with the woman I love, that's all. Now if you are done asking me all these questions, can we please board this airplane, so we can go and have some fun?"

"Okay, let's go but I still believe you are up to something. A woman's intuition is never wrong."

"Are you suggesting that the Holy Spirit is a woman's intuition?"

"Ha, ha! What are you now, a comedian? Charles please keep your day job and leave the jokes to those who are anointed to bring laughter to others," Jasmine answered.

"Jasmine, I was not trying to be funny when I said that, I was simply asking a question. Alright let's get off that subject and get on this plane."

"Yes, you're right. Let's get off that subject and on this plane before I get mad at you."

Nevertheless, Jasmine and Charles boarded the airplane and spent the next few hours flying to an island paradise. After being in the air for nearly three hours, Jasmine and Charles finally landed on Turks and Caicos Island.

Once they got off the airplane, they retrieved their luggage, found a taxi and went to their resort. As their taxi pulled on the grounds of the resort, they were mesmerized by what they saw.

"Oh my, Charles you did an excellent job picking this place for us. If it's this beautiful outside, I can only image how it looks in the rooms."

"Nothing but the best for the love of my life. Jasmine before we check-in I want you to be aware that I booked connecting rooms for us. I wanted to minimize the onset of temptation between the two of us. And you don't have to worry about anything this week, I'm paying for our stay."

"Charles, that's so sweet of you. I still don't know why you love me so much."

Without Jasmine understanding what Charles said, he murmured," but tonight you will."

"Charles, did you say something?" "No sweetie. I didn't say anything. Let's check-in."

From the moment Jasmine and Charles checked into their resort suites, Charles ran around, secretly preparing a romantic evening for Jasmine. Meanwhile, Jasmine took advantage of the plush comfortable bed in her room and took a nap. After Charles had finalized his plans for a romantic evening with Jasmine, he realized that he forgot to call Peggy to let her know that he and Jasmine made it to the islands safely.

Hence, Charles called Peggy and informed her that he and Jasmine made it to their destination. Afterward he went to Jasmine's room, but she didn't answer the door, so he assumed that she was taking a nap and thought it would be wise if he did the same. When Charles woke up, he called Jasmine's room to see if she was up to inform her that he had made a reservation for them to have dinner on the beach.

"Hey sleeping beauty, you up?" "You woke me up, so I guess I am."

"I hope you had a restful nap. I wanted to let you know that I made a seven-thirty dinner reservation tonight for us, so please be ready." "Okay, I'll be ready."

As soon as Charles got off the phone with Jasmine, he quickly got dressed and rushed to the resort gift shop before they closed to purchase some flowers and a small ceramic seahorse, Jasmine's favorite sea animal. Since Charles was already in the lobby of the resort, he called Jasmine's room and told her to meet him in the lobby. When Jasmine arrived in the lobby, she asked Charles where they were going for dinner. He told her it was a surprise. As Jasmine and Charles walked throughout the resort, Jasmine continued to ask Charles where they were going, and he continuously told her it was a surprise. After about ten minutes of walking, Charles and Jasmine finally arrived at the spot where they would eat. Just as Charles promised Jasmine, the scenery of the beach setting impressed her.

"Ah Charles is this where we are having dinner? When did you have time to set all of this up?"

"Yes, my love, we are having dinner here and I did it all while you were sleeping."

When Charles proceeded to pull Jasmine's seat out so that she could sit down, Jasmine kissed him on the cheek. Shortly thereafter, the waiter assigned to Charles and Jasmine's table took their drink and food orders. While they waited for their drink and appetizers to arrive, they sat and chatted.

Within ten-minutes the waters, stuffed mushrooms and spinach dip, Charles and Jasmine had ordered, arrived. The entire time they snacked on their appetizers, Charles nervously looked at his watch wondering when it would be the right time to propose to Jasmine.

Then Charles thought to himself, "It's now or never. Here goes nothing." Charles gently grabbed Jasmine's hand, took a deep breath and said, "Jasmine, since the first time I met you at the youth retreat when my family attended New Life Holiness Church, I knew then I wanted you in my life. Now, after all these years of waiting, here you are with me on the beach in the Turks and Caicos Islands."

"Charles, what's the matter?" "Please Jasmine let me finish." "I'm sorry, go ahead."

"Jasmine, you are the type of woman I see myself raising children and growing old with. Jasmine, I don't want to go another day, month, or year without you in my life. What I'm trying to say is, Jasmine will you do me the honor and become my wife?"

After hearing what Charles said, Jasmine sat stunned and unable to speak. "Jasmine will you marry me?"

Jasmine bust out in tears and said, "Yes Charles. Yes, I will marry you."

When Charles heard the word yes come out of Jasmine's mouth, he picked her up and yelled to the top of his lungs in excitement.

"Charles, what about my mother? Do you think she will approve of us getting married?"

"No worries, I've already had a full discussion with your mother before I left Swainsboro and she gave me her blessing. Oops, I almost forgot here's your ring, let me put it on your finger."

Charles put on his fiancée's engagement ring on her finger, as she stated, "Oh my gosh, we are getting married!" Jasmine and Charles spent the rest of their time on Turks and Caicos Islands enjoying site seeing, scuba diving, and relaxing around the resort's pool.

CHAPTER 36

It would seem as though Jasmine had reached the pinnacle of success in her life. She had formed a personal relationship with God, discovered the true meaning to life, gained a sense of purpose and was now engaged to the love of her life. Sadly, this jovial moment in Jasmine's life was short lived because she found out that her mother Peggy had fallen-ill.

For the second time in her adult life, Jasmine had to return home to help take care of a sick parent. Although, Jasmine was willing to go home to assist with her mother's care, she didn't know it would be long-term care.

The day after Jasmine found out that her mother was sick, she called Charles to inform him of what was happening and to let him know that she would be coming home for an extended period to help with her mother. Being the supportive person Charles had always been with Jasmine, he told her that everything concerning her mother was going to work-out and that God would get the glory.

Jasmine agreed and told Charles that she would see him in the next few days. Before Jasmine and Charles ended their call, they told one another that they loved each other. For the next two days Jasmine spent time at work scheduling project assignments for her team, packing and paying her bills.

Nevertheless, days later Jasmine arrived in Swainsboro and soon as she got in town, she immediately went to the hospital to see about her mother. When she got to her mother's room, she noticed her sister's talking to their mother's doctor. As Jasmine walked toward her sisters and the doctor, she observed how they were looking at her, so she decided to find out what was going on with her mother.

"Hi Ashley and Allison, how's mom?", Jasmine inquired.

"Hey, we just found out that she's not doing well at all. They're saying that we need to consider placing her in hospice care. And you know mom wouldn't want that," Allison suggested.

"What does mom have to say about being under hospice care?", Jasmine asked.

"She says she doesn't want it, she wants one of us to take care of her," Ashley replied.

"Do you think that would be wise? None of us have medical training," Jasmine stated.

"Well Jasmine, Ashley and I discussed it before you got here, and we think that it would be best if you moved back here and take care of mom," Allison answered.

"You know I wouldn't mind doing it because after all she is our mother, but it would have been nice if the both of you included me in the decision-making process. I'll need to talk to Charles and see what he says before I agree to this arrangement."

"Why do you feel like you need to discuss a family issue with him?", Ashley inquired.

"Maybe because he's about to be my husband and a decision like this will impact his life as well as my life," Jasmine responded.

Throughout the entire time that the Sawman daughters were outside Peggy's room talking they were unaware that she was awake and heard every word that they said. With the little strength Peggy had, she summoned her daughters to come into her room so she could talk to them.

"Allison and Ashely, I heard what the both of you just told Jasmine and want you two to know it's not fair to her. The last time I checked I had three children, not just one. Jasmine was right when she said she needed to discuss with Charles everything that's going on with me. He's soon to be her husband, so it's up to the two of them what Jasmine does from here on out."

The next few words that came out of Peggy's mouth shocked everyone in the room, especially Jasmine. "Jasmine, I know you and Charles have been planning your wedding for the past few months. I want to ask you a big favor?" "What's that mom?"

"Would you consider getting married the day after tomorrow?", Peggy asked. "Mom, why so soon?"

"I don't know if I will live long enough to make it to your wedding. I just want to make sure I was present the day you said *I do* to the person you love."

"Okay, I'll call Charles and discuss it with him and see what he says."

As promised Jasmine called Charles and shared with him what her mother requested.

Realizing that no one, including the doctors, didn't know how long Peggy had to live, Charles agreed with Jasmine that they would get married in the next two days.

Fortunately, Jasmine and Charles had no problem with obtaining a marriage license and arranging for the Rev. Dr. Peterson to officiate the wedding and Charles' parents and siblings to witness it. As it would be Peggy was right to ask her daughter to speed up her nuptials because a few hours after Jasmine and Charles said I do, Peggy passed away unexpectedly. It was sad the way Jasmine and Charles' marriage commenced, yet to them it was worth it, because Peggy finally got to see her baby girl reach a place of wholeness in her life by marrying someone who loved and adored her.

The love that Jasmine finally found with Charles is the kind of love every young woman hopes and dreams to experience one time in their life. However, they never understand what they must surrender to obtain it; their past mistakes, the loss of loved ones and the yearning of their will for God's will for their life.

BOOK CLUB DISCUSSION GUIDE

Dear Reader,

The following questions have been devcloped to help guide your book club discussion. The construct of these questions is based on the topics contained within each section of the novel. It is my hope that you will take the time to explore all the questions and gain a better understanding of each character.

Metamorphoses of a Young Girl

1. Why do you believe Jasmine was attracted to Dontrelle?
2. How did the dynamics of Dontrelle's family and environment possibly influence his behavior and the decisions he made in his life?
3. Why do you think Jasmine and Sheila's friendship formed so quickly?

The Change

4. Discuss why you think Jasmine's relationship with Dontrelle changed her behavior at home and school.
5. Based on the depiction of Peggy and Carl Sawman's parenting style, do you

think they were wrong with the standards they utilized to guide their daughters to become respectable young women?

6. Which rule enforced by Jasmine's parents do you think led her to become disrespectful?

Lost

7. Do you believe Jasmine unknowingly suffered from low self-esteem and that's why she wanted to have Dontrelle's baby?

Twisted Love

8. What reason do you believe Jasmine chose to date Isaac?

9. Is it commonplace for young ladies like Jasmine to become involved with an abusive mate early in life?

The Lust Factor

10. How has Curtis taken advantage of his position with the Centél Firm to fraternized with subordinates assigned to his team?

11. In what other ways could Jasmine have handled the situation with Curtis?

12. Should Jasmine have reported Curtis' advances toward her earlier to upper level management? If so, why?

Two Faces of Frenemies

13. What do you think is the rationale behind Reggie monitoring Jasmine's phone calls to her parents?
14. Do you think Sheila was jealous of Jasmine and that was the reason why she secretly dated Reggie behind her back?
15. How could Jasmine have better handled the situation with Sheila and Reggie, when she found out they were having an affair behind her back?

A Shade of Darkness

16. Do you think Jasmine blames herself for being raped by Damien? If so, explain.
17. Could fear be the reason why Jasmine took so long to report her rape to the authorities?
18. Why do you think Jasmine chose not to disclose to her parents that she had been raped?

Crossroads

19. Would you agree that it was necessary that Jasmine sought professional help to deal with being raped?
20. Do you think Jasmine's outlook on life improved or diminished after she began therapy with Dr. Boatman?

The Cross of Redemption

21. Do you feel Jasmine gained a sense of freedom from writing the forgiveness letter to herself? If so, explain?

A Beckon of Hope

22. Why do you think there's so much animosity between Jasmine and her sisters?
23. Do you think Peggy should have told Jasmine the reason why she wanted her children to come home?
24. Was Peggy justified in her response to Jasmine when she stated that she and her husband was always supportive of her throughout her challenges in life?

A Season of Recovery

25. Why do you think Jasmine strongly disagreed with Charles when he told her mother that they were going out on a dinner date?

26. What qualities does Charles possess that Jasmine seemed to not be fond of?

Love Defined

27. When Charles visited Jasmine, do you believe she intentionally tried to sabotage their relationship by comparing him with the men of her past?

Wholeness

28. In your opinion why do you think Jasmine had a difficult time believing that Charles truly loved her the way he said he did?

29. Would you agree that Peggy died in peace knowing that her daughter finally found true love?

BOOKS WRTTTEN BY
BESSIE STEWART-BANKS

ISBN-13: 978-0692888001

Bessie's testimony of healing and deliverance takes you on a journey through the pitfalls of losing a parent, a child and divorce to self-discovery and a restored relationship with God. In Finding Him I Found Me is an awe-aspiring story that will change the trajectory of your life and give you a new perspective.

Available at all major online bookstores, Kindle or visit https://www.booksbybessie.org

BOOKS WRTTTEN BY
BESSIE STEWART-BANKS

ISBN-13: 978-0692107720

Fear is the number one hindrance that stops many people from moving into their destiny, stepping out on faith to pursue their hopes and dreams, and valuing the uniqueness of others. In this spiritually-filled book you will discover some of the origins of fear, how it can impact your life and ways you can utilize to move toward faith in Christ Jesus.

Available at all major online bookstores, Kindle or visit https://www.booksbybessie.org

Ways to Connect with Author

To correspond with Dr. Bessie Stewart-Banks

send all inquiries to bessieban27@gmail.com.

or

To schedule speaking engagements, visit
https://www.booksbybessie.org/book-bessie

CONSCIOUS OF THE HEART PUBLISHING
"Let Us Breathe Life into Your Words"

Since its inception, Conscious of the Heart Publishing, LLC, has held a high standard for producing quality work and has made every attempt to exceed the expectation of its clients. Conscious of the Heart Publishing strives in its commitment to ensure that all clients of the company are treated with respect, dignity and a spirit of excellence.

We hope you enjoy this book released from Conscious of the Heart Publishing, LLC. Our goal is to provide inspirational and thought-provoking literature through a creative and expressive channel to affect change in the lives of our readers. For more information on other books and products focused on family, finance, relationships, personal growth, professional and spiritual development, go to www.cothpublishing.com or write to:

Conscious of the Heart Publishing, LLC

P.O. Box 1452

Redan, Georgia 30074